William Cullen Bryant

Thirty Poems

William Cullen Bryant

Thirty Poems

ISBN/EAN: 9783744707756

Printed in Europe, USA, Canada, Australia, Japan

Cover: Foto ©Andreas Hilbeck / pixelio.de

More available books at **www.hansebooks.com**

THIRTY POEMS

WILLIAM CULLEN BRYANT.

NEW YORK:
D. APPLETON AND COMPANY,
443 & 445 BROADWAY.
LONDON: 16 LITTLE BRITAIN.
M.DCCC.LXIV.

TO THE READER.

––––––––––

THE author has attempted no other classifi-
cation of the poems in this volume than that of
allowing them to follow each other according
to the order of time in which they were written. It has seemed to him that this arrange-
ment is as satisfactory as any other, since, at
different periods of life, an author's style and
habits of thought may be supposed to undergo
very considerable modifications. One poem

forms an exception to this order of succession, and should have appeared in an earlier collection. Three others have already appeared in an illustrated edition of the author's poems.

NEW YORK, *December*, 1863.

CONTENTS.

POEMS.

THE PLANTING OF THE APPLE TREE.

Come, let us plant the apple tree.
Cleave the tough greensward with the spade;
Wide let its hollow bed be made;
There gently lay the roots, and there
Sift the dark mould with kindly care,
  And press it o'er them tenderly,
As, round the sleeping infant's feet
We softly fold the cradle sheet;
  So plant we the apple tree.

What plant we in this apple tree?
Buds, which the breath of summer days
Shall lengthen into leafy sprays;
  1*

Boughs where the thrush, with crimson breast,
Shall haunt and sing and hide her nest;
   We plant, upon the sunny lea,
A shadow for the noontide hour,
A shelter from the summer shower,
   When we plant the apple tree.

   What plant we in this apple tree?
Sweets for a hundred flowery springs,
To load the May-wind's restless wings,
When, from the orchard row, he pours
Its fragrance through our open doors;
   A world of blossoms for the bee,
Flowers for the sick girl's silent room,
For the glad infant sprigs of bloom,
   'We plant with the apple tree.

   What plant we in this apple tree?
Fruits that shall swell in sunny June,
And redden in the August noon,

And drop, when gentle airs come by,
That fan the blue September sky,
　　While children come, with cries of glee,
And seek them where the fragrant grass
Betrays their bed to those who pass,
　　At the foot of the apple tree.

　　And when, above this apple tree,
The winter stars are quivering bright,
And winds go howling through the night,
Girls, whose young eyes o'erflow with mirth,
Shall peel its fruit by cottage hearth,
　　And guests in prouder homes shall see,
Heaped with the grape of Cintra's vine,
And golden orange of the line,
　　The fruit of the apple tree.

　　The fruitage of this apple tree
Winds, and our flag of stripe and star
Shall bear to coasts that lie afar,

Where men shall wonder at the view,
And ask in what fair groves they grew ;
    And sojourners beyond the sea
Shall think of childhood's careless day,
And long, long hours of summer play,
    In the shade of the apple tree.

    Each year shall give this apple tree
A broader flush of roseate bloom,
A deeper maze of verdurous gloom,
And loosen, when the frost-clouds lower,
The crisp brown leaves in thicker shower.
    The years shall come and pass, but we
Shall hear no longer, where we lie,
The summer's songs, the autumn's sigh,
    In the boughs of the apple tree.

    And time shall waste this apple tree.
Oh, when its aged branches throw
Thin shadows on the ground below,

Shall fraud and force and iron will
Oppress the weak and helpless still ?
　What shall the tasks of mercy be,
Amid the toils, the strifes, the tears
Of those who live when length of years,
　Is wasting this apple tree ?

" Who planted this old apple tree ? "
The children of that distant day
Thus to some aged man shall say ;
And gazing on its mossy stem,
The gray-haired man shall answer them :
" A poet of the land was he,
Born in the rude but good old times ;
'Tis said he made some quaint old rhymes
　On planting the apple tree."

THE SNOW-SHOWER.

Stand here by my side and turn, I pray,
  On the lake below thy gentle eyes;
The clouds hang over it, heavy and gray,
  And dark and silent the water lies;
And out of that frozen mist the snow
In wavering flakes begins to flow;
              Flake after flake,
They sink in the dark and silent lake.

See how in a living swarm they come
  From the chambers beyond that misty veil;
Some hover awhile in air, and some
  Rush prone from the sky like summer hail.

All, dropping swiftly or settling slow,
Meet, and are still in the depths below;
         Flake after flake
Dissolved in the dark and silent lake.

Here delicate snow-stars, out of the cloud,
  Come floating downward in airy play,
Like spangles dropped from the glistening
    crowd
  That whiten by night the milky way;
There broader and burlier masses fall;
The sullen water buries them all—
         Flake after flake—
All drowned in the dark and silent lake.

And some, as on tender wings they glide
  From their chilly birth-cloud, dim and gray,
Are joined in their fall, and, side by side,
  Come clinging along their unsteady way;

As friend with friend, or husband with wife
Makes hand in hand the passage of life ;
Each mated flake
Soon sinks in the dark and silent lake.

Lo ! while we are gazing, in swifter haste
  Stream down the snows, till the air is white,
As, myriads by myriads madly chased,
  They fling themselves from their shadowy
    height.   .
The fair, frail creatures of middle sky,
What speed they make, with their grave so
    nigh ;
Flake after flake,
To lie in the dark and silent lake !

I see in thy gentle eyes a tear ;
  They turn to me in sorrowful thought ;
Thou thinkest of friends, the good and dear,
  Who were for a time and now are not ;

Like these fair children of cloud and frost,
That glisten a moment and then are lost,
   Flake after flake—
All lost in the dark and silent lake.

Yet look again, for the clouds divide;
 A gleam of blue on the water lies;
And far away, on the mountain-side,
 A sunbeam falls from the opening skies.
But the hurrying host that flew between
The cloud and the water, no more is seen;
   Flake after flake,
At rest in the dark and silent lake.

A RAIN DREAM.

THESE strifes, these tumults of the noisy world,
Where Fraud, the coward, tracks his prey by
     stealth,
And Strength, the ruffian, glories in his guilt,
Oppress the heart with sadness. Oh, my friend,
In what serener mood we look upon
The gloomiest aspects of the elements
Among the woods and fields ! Let us awhile,
As the slow wind is rolling up the storm,
In fancy leave this maze of dusty streets,
For ever shaken by the importunate jar
Of commerce, and upon the darkening air
Look from the shelter of our rural home.

Who is not awed that listens to the Rain,
Sending his voice before him ? Mighty Rain !
The upland steeps are shrouded by thy mists ;
Thy shadow fills the hollow vale ; the pools
No longer glimmer, and the silvery streams
Darken to veins of lead at thy approach.
Oh, mighty Rain ! already thou art here ;
And every roof is beaten by thy streams,
And, as thou passest, every glassy spring
Grows rough, and every leaf in all the woods
Is struck, and quivers. All the hill-tops slake
Their thirst from thee ; a thousand languishing
    fields,
A thousand fainting gardens, are refreshed ;
A thousand idle rivulets start to speed,
And with the graver murmur of the storm
Blend their light voices as they hurry on.
    Thou fill'st the circle of the atmosphere
Alone ; there is no living thing abroad,
No bird to wing the air nor beast to walk
The field : the squirrel in the forest seeks

His hollow tree; the marmot of the field
Has scampered to his den : the butterfly
Hides under her broad leaf; the insect crowds
That made the sunshine populous, lie close
In their mysterious shelters, whence the sun
Will summon them again.   The mighty Rain
Holds the vast empire of the sky alone.

    I shut my eyes, and see, as in a dream,
The friendly clouds drop down spring violets
And summer columbines, and all the flowers
That tuft the woodland floor, or overarch
The streamlet :—spiky grass for genial June,
Brown harvests for the waiting husbandman,
And for the woods a deluge of fresh leaves.

    I see these myriad drops that slake the dust,
Gathered in glorious streams, or rolling blue
In billows on the lake or on the deep
And bearing navies.   I behold them change
To threads of crystal as they sink in earth
And leave its stains behind, to rise again
In pleasant nooks of verdure, where the child,

Thirsty with play, in both his little hands
Shall take the cool, clear water, raising it
To wet his pretty lips.   To-morrow noon
How proudly will the water-lily ride
The brimming pool, o'erlooking, like a queen,
Her circle of broad leaves.   In lonely wastes,
When next the sunshine makes them beautiful,
Gay troops of butterflies shall light to drink
At the replenished hollows of the rock.
    Now slowly falls the dull blank night, and
      still,
All through the starless hours, the mighty Rain
Smites with perpetual sound the forest leaves,
And beats the matted grass, and still the earth
Drinks the unstinted bounty of the clouds—
Drinks for her cottage wells, her woodland
      brooks—
Drinks for the springing trout, the toiling bee
And brooding bird—drinks for her tender
      flowers,
Tall oaks, and all the herbage of her hills.

A melancholy sound is in the air,
A deep sigh in the distance, a shrill wail
Around my dwelling.   'Tis the wind of night;
A lonely wanderer between earth and cloud,
In the black shadow and the chilly mist,
Along   the   streaming   mountain   side,   and
      through
The dripping woods, and o'er the plashy fields,
Roaming and sorrowing still, like one who
      makes
The journey of life alone, and nowhere meets
A welcome or a friend, and still goes on
In darkness.   Yet awhile, a little while,
And he shall toss the glittering leaves in play,
And dally with the flowers, and gaily lift
The slender herbs, pressed low by weight of
      rain,
And drive, in joyous triumph, through the sky,
White clouds, the laggard remnants of the
      storm.

ROBERT OF LINCOLN.

MERRILY swinging on briar and weed,
   Near to the nest of his little dame,
Over the mountain-side or mead,
   Robert of Lincoln is telling his name :
        . Bob-o'-link, bob-o'-link,
        Spink, spank, spink ;
Snug and safe is that nest of ours,
Hidden among the summer flowers.
                Chee, chee, chee.

Robert of Lincoln is gaily drest,
   Wearing a bright black wedding coat ;
White are his shoulders and white his crest,
   Hear him call in his merry note :

Bob-o'-link, bob-o'-link,
Spink, spank, spink ;
Look, what a nice new coat is mine,
Sure there was never a bird so fine.
     Chee, chee, chee.

Robert of Lincoln's Quaker wife,
 Pretty and quiet, with plain brown wings,
Passing at home a patient life,
 Broods in the grass while her husband sings :
  Bob-o'-link, bob-o'-link,
  Spink, spank, spink ;
Brood, kind creature ; you need not fear
Thieves and robbers while I am here.
     Chee, chee, chee.

Modest and shy as a nun is she ;
 One weak chirp is her only note.
Braggart and prince of braggarts is he,
 Pouring boasts from his little throat :

Bob-o'-link, bob-o'-link,
Spink, spank, spink;
Never was I afraid of man;
Catch me, cowardly knaves, if you can.
Chee, chee, chee.

Six white eggs on a bed of hay,
Flecked with purple, a pretty sight!
There as the mother sits all day,
Robert is singing with all his might:
Bob-o'-link, bob-o'-link,
Spink, spank, spink;
Nice, good wife, that never goes out,
Keeping house while I frolic about.
Chee, chee, chee.

Soon as the little ones chip the shell
Six wide mouths are open for food;
Robert of Lincoln bestirs him well,
Gathering seeds for the hungry brood.

2

Bob-o'-link, bob-o'-link,
Spink, spank, spink;
This new life is likely to be
Hard for a gay young fellow like me.
                    Chee, chee, chee.

Robert of Lincoln at length is made
    Sober with work, and silent with care;
Off is his holiday garment laid,
    Half forgotten that merry air,
        Bob-o'-link, bob-o'-link,
        Spink, spank, spink;
Nobody knows but my mate and I
Where our nest and our nestlings lie.
                    Chee, chee, chee.

Summer wanes; the children are grown;
    Fun and frolic no more he knows;
Robert of Lincoln's a humdrum crone;
    Off he flies, and we sing as he goes:

Bob-o'-link, bob-o'-link,
Spink, spank, spink;
When you can pipe that merry old strain,
Robert of Lincoln, come back again.
Chee, chee, chee.

THE TWENTY-SEVENTH OF MARCH.

Oh, gentle one, thy birthday sun should rise
Amid a chorus of the merriest birds
That ever sang the stars out of the sky
In a June morning. Rivulets should send
A voice of gladness from their winding paths,
Deep in o'erarching grass, where playful winds,
Stirring the loaded stems should shower the,
    dew
Upon the glassy water. Newly blown
Roses, by thousands, to the garden walks
Should tempt the loitering moth and diligent
    bee.
The longest, brightest day in all the year

Should be the day on which thy cheerful eyes
First opened on the earth, to make thy haunts
Fairer and gladder for thy kindly looks.
    Thus might a poet say; but I must bring
A birthday offering of an humbler strain,
And yet it may not please thee less.   I hold
That 'twas the fitting season for thy birth
When March, just ready to depart, begins
To soften into April.   Then we have
The delicatest and most welcome flowers,
And yet they take least heed of bitter wind
And lowering sky.   The periwinkle then,
In an hour's sunshine, lifts her azure blooms
Beside the cottage door; within the woods
Tufts of ground-laurel, creeping underneath
The leaves of the last summer, send their sweets
Up to the chilly air; and, by the oak,
The squirrel-cups, a graceful company,
Hide in their bells a soft aërial blue—
Sweet flowers, that nestle in the humblest
        nooks,

And yet within whose smallest bud is wrapt
A world of promise! Still the north wind
    breathes
His frost, and still the sky sheds snow and sleet;
Yet ever, when the sun looks forth again,
The flowers smile up to him from their low
    seats.
  Well hast thou borne the bleak March day of
    life.
Its storms and its keen winds to thee have been
Most kindly tempered, and through all its gloom
There has been warmth and sunshine in thy
    heart;
The griefs of life to thee have been like snows,
That light upon the fields in early spring,
Making them greener. In its milder hours,
The smile of this pale season, thou hast seen,
The glorious bloom of June, and in the note
Of early bird, that comes a messenger
From climes of endless verdure, thou hast
    heard

The choir that fills the summer woods with
    song.
  Now be the hours that yet remain to thee
Stormy or sunny, sympathy and love,
That inextinguishably dwell within
Thy heart, shall give a beauty and a light
To the most desolate moments, like the glow
Of a bright fireside in the wildest day ;
And kindly words and offices of good
Shall wait upon thy steps, as thou goest on,
Where God shall lead thee, till thou reach the
    gates
Of a more genial season, and thy path
Be lost to human eye among the bowers
And living fountains of a brighter land.

    Written *March*, 1855.

AN INVITATION TO THE COUNTRY.

ALREADY, close by our summer dwelling,
  The Easter sparrow repeats her song ;
A merry warbler, she chides the blossoms—
  The idle blossoms that sleep so long.

The blue-bird chants, from the elm's long
      branches,
  A hymn to welcome the budding year.
The south wind wanders from field to forest,
  And softly whispers : the Spring is here.

Come, daughter mine, from the gloomy city,
  Before those lays from the elm have ceased ;
The violet breathes, by our door, as sweetly
  As in the air of her native East.

Though many a flower in the wood is waking,
   The daffodil is our doorside queen;
She pushes upward the sward already,
   To spot with sunshine the early green.

No lays so joyous as these are warbled
   From wiry prison in maiden's bower;
No pampered bloom of the greenhouse cham-
      ber
   Has half the charm of the lawn's first flower.

Yet these sweet sounds of the early season,
   And these fair sights of its sunny days
Are only sweet when we fondly listen,
   And only fair when we fondly gaze.

There is no glory in star or blossom,
   Till looked upon by a loving eye;
There is no fragrance in April breezes,
   Till breathed with joy as they wander by.

2*

Come, Julia dear, for the sprouting willows,
　The opening flowers, and the gleaming
　　brooks,
And hollows, green in the sun, are waiting
　Their dower of beauty from thy glad looks.

A SONG FOR NEW YEAR'S EVE.

Stay yet, my friends, a moment stay—
    Stay till the good old year,
So long companion of our way,
    Shakes hands, and leaves us here.
        Oh stay, oh stay,
One little hour, and then away.

The year, whose hopes were high and strong,
    Has now no hopes to wake ;
Yet one hour more of jest and song
    For his familiar sake.
        Oh stay, oh stay,
One mirthful hour, and then away.

The kindly year, his liberal hands
   Have lavished all his store.
And shall we turn from where he stands,
   Because he gives no more?
     Oh stay, oh stay,
One grateful hour, and then away.

Days brightly came and calmly went,
   While yet he was our guest;
How cheerfully the week was spent!
   How sweet the seventh day's rest!
     Oh stay, oh stay,
One golden hour, and then away.

Dear friends were with us, some who sleep
   Beneath the coffin lid:
What pleasant memories we keep
   Of all they said and did!
     Oh stay, oh stay,
One tender hour, and then away.

Even while we sing he smiles his last
  And leaves our sphere behind.
The good old year is with the past;
  Oh be the new as kind !
    Oh stay, oh stay,
One parting strain, and then away.

THE WIND AND STREAM.

A BROOK came stealing from the ground ;
  You scarcely saw its silvery gleam
Among the herbs that hung around
  The borders of that winding stream,
The pretty stream, the placid stream,
The softly gliding, bashful stream.

A breeze came wandering from the sky,
  Light as the whispers of a dream ;
He put the o'erhanging grasses by,
  And softly stooped to kiss the stream,
The pretty stream, the flattered stream,
The shy, yet unreluctant stream.

The water, as the wind passed o'er,
   Shot upward many a glancing beam,
Dimpled and quivered more and more,
   And tripped along, a livelier stream.
The flattered stream, the simpering stream,
The fond, delighted, silly stream.

Away the airy wanderer flew
   To where the fields with blossoms teem,
To sparkling springs and rivers blue,
   And left alone that little stream,
The flattered stream, the cheated stream,
The sad, forsaken, lonely stream.

That careless wind came never back ;
   He wanders yet the fields I deem,
But, on its melancholy track,
   Complaining went that little stream,
The cheated stream, the hopeless stream,
The ever-murmuring, mourning stream.

THE LOST BIRD.

From the Spanish of CAROLINA CORONADO DE PERRY.

My bird has flown away,
Far out of sight has flown, I know not where.
Look in your lawn, I pray,
Ye maidens, kind and fair,
And see if my beloved bird be there.

His eyes are full of light;
The eagle of the rock has such an eye;
And plumes, exceeding bright,

Round his smooth temples lie,
And sweet his voice and tender as a sigh.

Look where the grass is gay
With summer blossoms, haply there he cowers;
  · And search, from spray to spray,
The leafy laurel bowers,
For well he loves the laurels and the flowers.

Find him, but do not dwell,
With eyes too fond, on the fair form you see,
Nor love his song too well;
Send him, at once, to me,
Or leave him to the air and liberty.

For only from my hand
He takes the seed into his golden beak,
And all unwiped shall stand
The tears that wet my cheek,
Till I have found the wanderer I seek.

My sight is darkened o'er,
Whene'er I miss his eyes, which are my day,
And when I hear no more
The music of his lay,
My heart in utter sadness faints away.

THE NIGHT JOURNEY OF A RIVER.

Oh River, gentle River! gliding on
In silence underneath this starless sky!
Thine is a ministry that never rests
Even while the living slumber.   For a time
The meddler, man, hath left the elements
In peace; the ploughman breaks the clods no
      more;
The miner labors not, with steel and fire,
To rend the rock, and he that hews the stone,
And he that fells the forest, he that guides
The loaded wain, and the poor animal
That drags it, have forgotten, for a time,
Their toils, and share the quiet of the earth.
    Thou pausest not in thine allotted task,

Oh darkling River! Through the night I hear
Thy wavelets rippling on the pebbly beach;
I hear thy current stir the rustling sedge,
That skirts thy bed; thou intermittest not
Thine everlasting journey, drawing on
A silvery train from many a woodland spring,
And mountain brook. The dweller by thy side,
Who moored his little boat upon thy beach,
Though all the waters that upbore it then
Have slid away o'er night, shall find, at morn,
Thy channel filled with waters freshly drawn
From distant cliffs and hollows where the rill
Comes up amid the water-flags. All night
Thou givest moisture to the thirsty roots
Of the lithe willow and o'erhanging plane,
And cherishest the herbage of thy bank,
Spotted with little flowers, and sendest up
Perpetually, the vapors from thy face,
To steep the hills with dew, or darken heaven
With drifting clouds, that trail the shadowy
        shower.

Oh River! darkling River! what a voice
Is that thou utterest while all else is still—
The ancient voice that, centuries ago,
Sounded between thy hills, while Rome was yet
A weedy solitude by Tiber's stream.
How many, at this hour, along thy course,
Slumber to thine eternal murmurings,
That mingle with the utterance of their dreams!
At dead of night the child awakes and hears
Thy soft, familiar dashings, and is soothed,
And sleeps again.   An airy multitude
Of little echoes, all unheard by day,
Faintly repeat, till morning, after thee,
The story of thine endless goings forth.
   Yet there are those who lie beside thy bed
For whom thou once didst rear the bowers that
     screen
Thy margin, and didst water the green fields;
And now there is no night so still that they
Can hear thy lapse; their slumbers, were thy
     voice

Louder than ocean's, it could never break.
For them the early violet no more
Opens upon thy bank, nor, for their eyes,
Glitter the crimson pictures of the clouds,
Upon thy bosom, when the sun goes down.
Their memories are abroad, the memories
Of those who last were gathered to the earth,
Lingering within the homes in which they sat,
Hovering above the paths in which they walked,
Haunting them like a presence. Even now
They visit many a dreamer in the forms
They walked in, ere at last they wore the
    shroud.
And eyes there are which will not close to
    dream,
For weeping and for thinking of the grave,
The new-made grave, and the pale one within.
These memories and these sorrows all shall fade,
And pass away, and fresher memories
And newer sorrows come and dwell awhile,
Beside thy borders, and, in turn, depart.

On glide thy waters, till at last they flow
Beneath the windows of the populous town,
And all night long give back the gleam of
    lamps,
And glimmer with the trains of light that
    stream
From halls where dancers whirl. A dimmer ray
Touches thy surface from the silent room
In which they tend the sick, or gather round
The dying; and a slender, steady beam
Comes from the little chamber, in the roof
Where, with a feverous crimson on her cheek,
The solitary damsel, dying, too,
Plies the quick needle till the stars grow pale.
There, close beside the haunts of revel, stand
The blank, unlighted windows, where the poor,
In hunger and in darkness, wake till morn.
There, drowsily, on the half conscious ear
Of the dull watchman, pacing on the wharf,
Falls the soft ripple of the waves that strike
On the moored bark; but guiltier listeners

Are nigh, the prowlers of the night, who steal
From shadowy nook to shadowy nook, and start
If other sounds than thine are in the air.

    Oh, glide away from those abodes, that bring
Pollution to thy channel and make foul
Thy once clear current; summon thy quick
    waves
And dimpling eddies; linger not, but haste,
With all thy waters, haste thee to the deep,
There to be tossed by shifting winds and rocked
By that mysterious force which lives within
The sea's immensity, and wields the weight
Of its abysses, swaying to and fro
The billowy mass, until the stain, at length,
Shall wholly pass away, and thou regain
The crystal brightness of thy mountain springs.

THE LIFE THAT IS.

THOU, who so long hast pressed the couch of
    pain,
    Oh welcome, welcome back to life's free
        breath—
To life's free breath and day's sweet light
    again,
    From the chill shadows of the gate of death.

For thou hadst reached the twilight bound be-
    tween
    The world of spirits and this grosser sphere;
Dimly by thee the things of earth were seen,
    And faintly fell earth's voices on thine ear.

3

And now, how gladly we behold, at last,
    The wonted smile returning to thy brow;
The very wind's low whisper, breathing past,
    In the light leaves, is music to thee now.

Thou wert not weary of thy lot; the earth
    Was ever good and pleasant in thy sight;
Still clung thy loves about the household
        hearth,
    And sweet was every day's returning light.

Then welcome back to all thou would'st not
        leave,
    To this grand march of seasons, days and
        hours;
The glory of the morn, the glow of eve,
    The beauty of the streams, and stars, and
        flowers;

To eyes on which thine own delight to rest;
    To voices which it is thy joy to hear;

To the kind toils that ever pleased thee best,
　The willing tasks of love, that made life
　　dear.

Welcome to grasp of friendly hands; to prayers
　Offered where crowds in reverent worship
　　come,
Or softly breathed amid the tender cares
　And loving inmates of thy quiet home.

Thou bring'st no tidings of the better land,
　Even from its verge; the mysteries opened
　　there
Are what the faithful heart may understand
　In its still depths, yet words may not de-
　　clare.

And well I deem, that, from the brighter side
　Of life's dim border, some o'erflowing rays
Streamed from the inner glory, shall abide
　Upon thy spirit through the coming days.

Twice wert thou given me; once in thy fair
    prime,
  Fresh from the fields of youth, when first
      we met,
And all the blossoms of that hopeful time
  Clustered and glowed where'er thy steps
      were set.

And now, in thy ripe autumn, once again
  Given back to fervent prayers and yearnings
      strong,
From the drear realm of sickness and of pain,
  When we had watched, and feared, and
      trembled long.

Now may we keep thee from the balmy air
  And radiant walks of heaven a little space,
Where He, who went before thee to prepare
  For His meek followers, shall assign thy
      place.

CASTELLAMARE, *May*, 1858.

SONG.

These prairies glow with flowers,
　　These groves are tall and fair,
The sweet lay of the mocking bird
　　Rings in the morning air ;
And yet I pine to see
　　My native hill once more,
And hear the sparrow's friendly chirp
　　Beside its cottage door.

And he, for whom I left
　　My native hill and brook,
Alas, I sometimes think I trace
　　A coldness in his look.

If I have lost his love
   I know my heart will break ;
And haply, they I left for him
   Will sorrow for my sake.

A SICK-BED.

Long hast thou watched my bed,
   And smoothed the pillow oft
For this poor, aching head,
   With touches kind and soft.

Oh ! smooth it yet again,
   As softly as before;
Once—only once—and then
   I need thy hand no more.

Yet here I may not stay,
   Where I so long have lain,

Through many a restless day,
　　And many a night of pain.

But bear me gently forth
　　Beneath the open sky,
Where, on the pleasant earth,
　　Till night the sunbeams lie.

There, through the coming days,
　　I shall not look to thee
My weary side to raise,
　　And shift it tenderly.

There sweetly shall I sleep ;
　　Nor wilt thou need to bring
And put to my hot lip
　　Cool water from the spring ;

Nor wet the kerchief laid
　　Upon my burning brow ;
Nor from my eyelids shade
　　The light that wounds them now ;

Nor watch that none shall tread,
  With noisy footstep, nigh ;
Nor listen by my bed,
  To hear my faintest sigh,

And feign a look of cheer,
  And words of comfort speak,
Yet turn to hide the tear
  That gathers on thy cheek.

Beside me, where I rest,
  Thy loving hands will set
The flowers that please me best :
  Moss-rose and violet.

Then to the sleep I crave
  Resign me, till I see
The face of Him who gave
  His life for thee and me.

Yet, with the setting sun,
  Come, now and then, at eve,
  3*

And think of me as one
   For whom thou should'st not grieve;

Who, when the kind release
   From sin and suffering came,
Passed to the appointed peace
   In murmuring thy name.

Leave at my side a space,
   Where thou shalt come, at last,
To find a resting place,
   When many years are past.

THE SONG OF THE SOWER.

THE maples redden in the sun ;
  In autumn gold the beeches stand ;
Rest, faithful plough, thy work is done
  Upon the teeming land.
Bordered with trees whose gay leaves fly
On every breath that sweeps the sky,
The fresh dark acres furrowed lie,
  And ask the sower's hand.
Loose the tired steer and let him go
To pasture where the gentians blow,
And we, who till the grateful ground,
Fling we the golden shower around.

II.

Fling wide the generous grain; we fling
O'er the dark mould the green of spring.
For thick the emerald blades shall grow,
When first the March winds melt the snow,
And to the sleeping flowers, below,
  The early bluebirds sing.
Fling wide the grain; we give the fields
 The ears that nod in summer's gale,
The shining stems that summer gilds,
 The harvest that o'erflows the vale,
And swells, an amber sea, between
The full-leaved woods, its shores of green.
Hark! from the murmuring clods I hear
Glad voices of the coming year;
The song of him who binds the grain,
The shout of those that load the wain,
And from the distant grange there comes
 The clatter of the thresher's flail,
And steadily the millstone hums
 Down in the willowy vale.

III.

Fling wide the golden shower; we trust
The strength of armies to the dust,
This peaceful lea may haply yield
Its harvest for the tented field.
Ha! feel ye not your fingers thrill,
   As o'er them, in the yellow grains,
Glide the warm drops of blood that fill
   For mortal strife, the warrior's veins;
Such as, on Solferino's day,
Slaked the brown sand and flowed away;—
Flowed till the herds, on Mincio's brink,
Snuffed the red stream and feared to drink;—
Blood that in deeper pools shall lie,
   On the sad earth, as time grows gray,
When men by deadlier arts shall die,
And deeper darkness blot the sky
    Above the thundering fray;
And realms, that hear the battle cry,
    Shall sicken with dismay;

And chieftains to the war shall lead
Whole nations, with the tempest's speed,
 To perish in a day ;—
Till man, by love and mercy taught,
Shall rue the wreck his fury wrought,
 And lay the sword away.
Oh strew, with pausing, shuddering hand,
The seed upon the helpless land,
As if, at every step, ye cast
The pelting hail and riving blast.

IV.

Nay, strew, with free and joyous sweep,
 The seed upon the expecting soil ;
For hence the plenteous year shall heap
 The garners of the men who toil.
Strew the bright seed for those who tear
The matted sward with spade and share,
And those whose sounding axes gleam
Beside the lonely forest stream,
 Till its broad banks lie bare ;

And him who breaks the quarry-ledge,
  With hammer-blows, plied quick and strong,
And him who, with the steady sledge,
  Smites the shrill anvil all day long.
Sprinkle the furrow's even trace
  For those whose toiling hands uprear
The roof-trees of our swarming race,
  By grove and plain, by stream and mere;
Who forth, from crowded city, lead
  The lengthening street, and overlay
Green orchard plot and grassy mead
  With pavement of the murmuring way.
Cast, with full hands, the harvest cast,
For the brave men that climb the mast,
When to the billow and the blast
  It swings and stoops, with fearful strain,
And bind the fluttering mainsail fast,
  Till the tossed bark shall sit, again,
  Safe as a seabird in the main.

V.

Fling wide the grain for those who throw
The clanking shuttle to and fro,
In the long row of humming rooms,
    And into ponderous masses wind
The web that, from a thousand looms,
    Comes forth to clothe mankind.
Strew, with free sweep, the grain for them,
    By whom the busy thread,
Along the garment's even hem
    And winding seam is led ;
A pallid sisterhood, that keep
    The lonely lamp alight,
In strife with weariness and sleep,
    Beyond the middle night.
Large part be theirs in what the year
Shall ripen for the reaper here.

VI.

Still, strew, with joyous hand, the wheat
On the soft mould beneath our feet,

For even now I seem
To hear a sound that lightly rings
From murmuring harp and viol's strings,
   As in a summer dream.
The welcome of the wedding guest,
  The bridegrooom's look of bashful pride,
  The faint smile of the pallid bride,
And bridemaid's blush at matron's jest,
And dance and song and generous dower
Are in the shining grains we shower.

VII.

Scatter the wheat for shipwrecked men,
Who, hunger-worn, rejoice again
  In the sweet safety of the shore,
And wanderers, lost in woodlands drear,
Whose pulses bound with joy to hear
  The herd's light bell once more.
  Freely the golden spray be shed
For him whose heart, when night comes down
On the close alleys of the town,
  Is faint for lack of bread.

In chill roof chambers, bleak and bare,
Or the damp cellar's stifling air,
She who now sees, in mute despair,
    Her children pine for food,
Shall feel the dews of gladness start
To lids long tearless, and shall part
The sweet loaf, with a grateful heart,
    Among her thin, pale brood.
Dear, kindly Earth, whose breast we till!
Oh, for thy famished children, fill,
    Where'er the sower walks,
Fill the rich ears that shade the mould
With grain for grain, a hundredfold,
    To bend the sturdy stalks.

VIII.

Strew silently the fruitful seed,
    As softly o'er the tilth ye tread,
For hands that delicately knead
    The consecrated bread.

The mystic loaf that crowns the board,
When, round the table of their Lord,
    Within a thousand temples set,
In memory of the bitter death
Of him who taught at Nazareth,
    His followers are met,
And thoughtful eyes with tears are wet,
    As of the Holy One they think,
The glory of whose rising, yet
    Makes bright the grave's mysterious brink.

IX.

    Brethren, the sower's task is done.
The seed is in its winter bed.
Now let the dark brown mould be spread,
    To hide it from the sun,
And leave it to the kindly care
Of the still earth and brooding air.
As when the mother, from her breast,
Lays the hushed babe apart to rest,
And shades its eyes and waits to see
How sweet its waking smile will be.

The tempest now may smite, the sleet
All night on the drowned furrow beat,
And winds that, from the cloudy hold,
Of winter breathe the bitter cold,
Stiffen to stone the mellow mould,
    Yet safe shall lie the wheat ;
Till, out of heaven's unmeasured blue,
  Shall walk again the genial year,
To wake with warmth and nurse with dew,
  The germs we lay to slumber here.

x.

Oh blessed harvest yet to be !
  Abide thou with the love that keeps,
In its warm bosom, tenderly,
  The life which wakes and that which sleeps.
The love that leads the willing spheres
Along the unending track of years,
And watches o'er the sparrow's nest,
Shall brood above thy winter rest,

And raise thee from the dust, to hold
   Light whisperings with the winds of May,
And fill thy spikes with living gold,
   From summer's yellow ray,
Then, as thy garners give thee forth,
   On what glad errands shalt thou go,
Wherever, o'er the waiting earth,
   Roads wind and rivers flow.
The ancient East shall welcome thee
To mighty marts beyond the sea,
And they who dwell where palm groves sound
To summer winds the whole year round,
Shall watch, in gladness, from the shore,
The sails that bring thy glistening store.

THE NEW AND THE OLD.

New are the leaves on the oaken spray,
   New the blades of the silky grass ;
Flowers, that were buds but yesterday,
   Peep from the ground where'er I pass.

These gay idlers, the butterflies,
   Broke, to-day, from their winter shroud,
These soft airs, that winnow the skies,
   Blow, just born, from the soft, white cloud.

Gushing fresh in the little streams
   What a prattle the waters make !

Even the sun, with his tender beams,
  Seems as young as the flowers they wake.

Children are wading, with cheerful cries,
  In the shoals of the sparkling brook,
Laughing maidens, with soft, young eyes,
  Walk or sit in the shady nook.

What am I doing, thus alone,
  In the glory of nature here,
Silver-haired, like a snow-flake thrown
  On the greens of the springing year?

Only for brows unploughed by care,
  Eyes that glisten with hope and mirth,
Cheeks unwrinkled, and unblanched hair,
  Shines this holiday of the earth.

Under the grass, with the clammy clay,
  Lie in darkness the last year's flowers,

Born of a light that has passed away,
  Dews long dried, and forgotten showers.

"Under the grass is the fitting home,"
  So they whisper, " for such as thou,
When the winter of life is come,
  Chilling the blood, and frosting the brow."

THE CLOUD ON THE WAY.

See before us, in our journey, broods a mist
    upon the ground;
Thither leads the path we walk in, blending
    with that gloomy bound.
Never eye hath pierced its shadows to the mys-
    tery they screen;
Those who once have passed within it never
    more on earth are seen.
Now it seems to stoop beside us, now at seem-
    ing distance lowers,
Leaving banks that tempt us onward bright
    with summer-green and flowers.

4

Yet it blots the way forever; there our journey
    ends at last;
Into that dark cloud we enter, and are gathered
    to the past.
Thou who, in this flinty pathway, leading
    through a stranger-land,
Passest down the rocky valley, walking with
    me hand in hand,
Which of us shall be the soonest folded to that
    dim Unknown?
Which shall leave the other walking in this
    flinty path alone?
Even now I see thee shudder, and thy cheek is
    white with fear,
And thou clingest to my side as comes that
    darkness sweeping near.
"Here," thou say'st, "the path is rugged, sown
    with thorns that wound the feet;
But the sheltered glens are lovely, and the riv-
    ulet's song is sweet;
Roses breathe from tangled thickets; lilies
    bend from ledges brown;

Pleasantly between the pelting showers the sun-
    shine gushes down;
Dear are those who walk beside us, they whose
    looks and voices make
All this rugged region cheerful, till I love it for
    their sake.
Far be yet the hour that takes me where that
    chilly shadow lies,
From the things I know and love and from the
    sight of loving eyes."
So thou murmurest, fearful one: but see, we
    tread a rougher way;
Fainter glow the gleams of sunshine that upon
    the dark rocks play;
Rude winds strew the faded flowers upon the
    crags o'er which we pass;
Banks of verdure, when we reach them, hiss
    with tufts of withered grass.
One by one we miss the voices which we loved
    so well to hear;
One by one the kindly faces in that shadow dis-
    appear.

Yet upon the mist before us fix thine eyes with
    closer view;

See, beneath its sullen skirts, the rosy morning
    glimmers through.

One whose feet the thorns have wounded passed
    that barrier and came back,

With a glory on His footsteps lighting yet the
    dreary track.

Boldly enter where He entered; all that seems
    but darkness here,

When thou hast passed beyond it, haply shall
    be crystal-clear.

Viewed from that serener realm, the walks of
    human life may lie,

Like the page of some familiar volume, open to
    thine eye;

Haply, from the overhanging shadow, thou
    may'st stretch an unseen hand,

To support the wavering steps that print with
    blood the rugged land.

Haply, leaning o'er the pilgrim, all unweeting
    thou art near,

Thou may'st whisper words of warning or of
    comfort in his ear,
Till, beyond the border where that brooding
    mystery bars the sight,
Those whom thou hast fondly cherished stand
    with thee in peace and light.

THE TIDES.

THE moon is at her full, and, riding high,
    Floods the calm fields with light.
The airs that hover in the summer sky
    Are all asleep to-night.

There comes no voice from the great woodlands
       round
    That murmured all the day ;
Beneath the shadow of their boughs, the ground
    Is not more still than they.

But ever heaves and moans the restless Deep ;
   His rising tides I hear,
Afar I see the glimmering billows leap ;
   I see them breaking near.

Each wave springs upward, climbing toward
    the fair
   Pure light that sits on high—
Springs eagerly, and faintly sinks, to where
   The mother waters lie.

Upward again it swells ; the moonbeams show,
   Again, its glimmering crest ;
Again it feels the fatal weight below,
   And sinks, but not to rest.

Again and yet again ; until the Deep
   Recalls his brood of waves ;
And, with a sullen moan, abashed, they creep
   Back to his inner caves.

Brief respite ! they shall rush from that recess
  With noise and tumult soon,
And fling themselves, with unavailing stress,
  Up toward the placid moon.

Oh, restless Sea, that, in thy prison here,
  Dost struggle and complain ;
Through the slow centuries yearning to be near
  To that fair orb in vain ;

The glorious source of light and heat must
    warm
  Thy billows from on high,
And change them to the cloudy trains that
    form
  The curtains of the sky.

Then only may they leave the waste of brine
  In which they welter here,
And rise above the hills of earth, and shine
  In a serener sphere.

ITALY.

Voices from the mountains speak;
  Apennines to Alps reply;
Vale to vale and peak to peak
  Toss an old remembered cry;
      Italy
      Shall be free!
  Such the mighty shout that fills
  All the passes of her hills.

All the old Italian lakes
  Quiver at that quickening word;
Como with a thrill awakes;
  Garda to her depths is stirred;

4*

Mid the steeps
Where he sleeps,
Dreaming of the elder years,
Startled Thrasymenus hears.

Sweeping Arno, swelling Po,
  Murmur freedom to their meads.
Tiber swift and Liris slow
  Send strange whispers from their reeds.
    Italy
    Shall be free,
Sing the glittering brooks that slide,
Toward the sea, from Etna's side.

Long ago was Gracchus slain;
  Brutus perished long ago;
Yet the living roots remain
  Whence the shoots of greatness grow.
    Yet again,
    God-like men,

Sprung from that heroic stem,
Call the land to rise with them.

They who haunt the swarming street,
    They who chase the mountain boar,
Or, where cliff and billow meet,
    Prune the vine or pull the oar,
        With a stroke
        Break their yoke;
Slaves but yestereve were they—
Freemen with the dawning day.

Looking in his children's eyes,
    While his own with gladness flash,
"These," the Umbrian father cries,
    "Ne'er shall crouch beneath the lash!
        These shall ne'er
        Brook to wear
Chains whose cruel links are twined
Round the crushed and withering mind."

Monarchs! ye whose armies stand
　　Harnessed for the battle-field!
Pause, and from the lifted hand
　　Drop the bolts of war ye wield.
　　　　Stand aloof
　　　　While the proof
Of the people's might is given ;
Leave their kings to them and heaven.

Stand aloof, and see the oppressed
　　Chase the oppressor, pale with fear,
As the fresh winds of the west
　　Blow the misty valleys clear.
　　　　Stand and see
　　　　Italy
Cast the gyves she wears no more
To the gulfs that steep her shore.

A DAY DREAM.

A DAY dream by the dark blue deep;
   Was it a dream, or something more?
I sat where Posilippo's steep,
   With its gray shelves, o'erhung the shore.

On ruined Roman walls around
   The poppy flaunted, for 'twas May;
And at my feet, with gentle sound,
   Broke the light billows of the bay.

I sat and watched the eternal flow
　　Of those smooth billows toward the shore,
While quivering lines of light below,
　　Ran with them on the ocean floor.

Till, from the deep, there seemed to rise
　　White arms upon the waves outspread,
Young faces, lit with soft blue eyes,
　　And smooth, round cheeks, just touched
　　　　with red.

Their long, fair tresses, tinged with gold,
　　Lay floating on the ocean streams,
And such their brows as bards behold—
　　Love-stricken bards, in morning dreams.

Then moved their coral lips; a strain
　　Low, sweet and sorrowful I heard,
As if the murmurs of the main
　　Were shaped to syllable and word.

"The sight thou dimly dost behold,
　　Oh, stranger from a distant sky!
Was often, in the days of old,
　　Seen by the clear, believing eye.

"Then danced we on the wrinkled sand,
　　Sat in cool caverns by the sea,
Or wandered up the bloomy land,
　　To talk with shepherds on the lea.

"To us, in storms, the seaman prayed,
　　And where our rustic altars stood,
His little children came and laid
　　The fairest flowers of field and wood,

"Oh woe, a long unending woe!
　　For who shall knit the ties again
That linked the sea-nymphs, long ago,
　　In kindly fellowship with men?

" Earth rears her flowers for us no more ;
  A half-remembered dream are we.
Unseen we haunt the sunny shore,
  And swim, unmarked, the glassy sea.

" And we have none to love or aid,
  But wander, heedless of mankind,
With shadows by the cloud-rack made,
  With moaning wave and sighing wind.

" Yet sometimes, as in elder days,
  We come before the painter's eye,
Or fix the sculptor's eager gaze,
  With no profaner witness nigh.

" And then the words of men grow warm
  With praise and wonder, asking where
The artist saw the perfect form
  He copied forth in lines so fair."

As thus they spoke, with wavering sweep
  Floated the graceful forms away;
Dimmer and dimmer, through the deep,
  I saw the white arms gleam and play.

Fainter and fainter, on mine ear,
  Fell the soft accents of their speech,
Till I, at last, could only hear
  The waves run murmuring up the beach.

THE RUINS OF ITALICA.

From the Spanish of Rioja.

I.

FABIUS, this region, desolate and drear,
  These solitary fields, this shapeless mound,
  Were once Italica, the far-renowned;
For Scipio, the mighty, planted here
His conquering colony, and now, o'erthrown,
Lie its once dreaded walls of massive stone.
      Sad relics, sad and vain,
      Of those invincible men
      Who held the region then.
Funereal memories alone remain
  Where forms of high example walked of yore.

Here lay the forum, there arose the fane,
    The eye beholds their places and no more.
Their proud gymnasium and their sumptuous
        baths,
Resolved to dust and cinders, strew the paths.
Their towers, that looked defiance at the sky,
Fallen by their own vast weight, in fragments
        lie.

II.

This broken circus, where the rock weeds climb,
    Flaunting with yellow blossoms, and defy
    The gods to whom its walls were piled so
        high,
Is now a tragic theatre, where Time
Acts his great fable, spreads a stage that shows
Past grandeur's story and its dreary close.
        Why, round this desert pit,
        Shout not the applauding rows
        Where the great people sit?
Wild beasts are here, but where the combatant,

With his bare arms, the strong athleta where?
All have departed from this once gay haunt
    Of noisy crowds, and silence holds the air.
Yet, on this spot, Time gives us to behold
A spectacle as stern as those of old.
As dreamily I gaze, there seem to rise,
From all the mighty ruin, wailing cries.

III.

The terrible in war, the pride of Spain,
    Trajan, his country's father, here was born;
Good, fortunate, triumphant, to whose reign
    Submitted the far regions, where the morn
Rose from her cradle, and the shore whose
        steeps
O'erlooked the conquered Gaditanian deeps.
        Of mighty Adrian here,
        Of Theodosius, saint,
        Of Silius, Virgil's peer,
Were rocked the cradles, rich with gold, and
        quaint

With ivory carvings; here were laurel boughs
And sprays of jasmine gathered for their
    brows,
    From gardens now a marshy, thorny
    waste.
Where rose the palace, reared for Cæsar, yawn
    Foul rifts to which the scudding lizards
    haste.
Palaces, gardens, Cæsars, all are gone,
And even the stones their names were graven
    on.

IV.

Fabius, if tears prevent thee not, survey
    The long dismantled streets, so thronged of
    old,
The broken marbles, arches in decay,
    Proud statues, toppled from their place and
    rolled
In dust, when Nemesis, the avenger, came,
    And buried, in forgetfulness profound,

The owners and their fame.
Thus Troy, I deem must be,
With many a mouldering mound;
And thou, whose name alone remains to thee,
Rome, of old gods and kings the native
    ground;
And thou, sage Athens, built by Pallas, whom
Just laws redeemed not from the appointed
    doom.
The envy of earth's cities once wert thou,—
A weary solitude and ashes now.
For fate and death respect ye not: they strike
The mighty city and the wise alike.

v.

But why goes forth the wandering thought to
    frame
  New themes of sorrow, sought in distant
    lands?
Enough the example that before me stands;
For here are smoke wreaths seen, and glimmer-
    ing flame,

And hoarse lamentings on the breezes die ;
So doth the mighty ruin cast its spell
  On those who near it dwell.
  And under night's still sky,
  As awe-struck peasants tell,
A melancholy voice is heard to cry,
" Italica is fallen ; " the echoes then
Mournfully shout " Italica" again.
  The leafy alleys of the forest nigh
  Murmur " Italica," and all around,
  A troop of mighty shadows, at the sound
Of that illustrious name, repeat the call,
" Italica ! " from ruined tower and wall.

WAITING BY THE GATE.

BESIDE a massive gateway built up in years gone
    by,
Upon whose top the clouds in eternal shadow
    lie,
While streams the evening sunshine on quiet
    wood and lea,
I stand and calmly wait till the hinges turn for
    me.

The tree tops faintly rustle beneath the breeze's
    flight,
A soft and soothing sound, yet it whispers of
    the night;

I hear the woodthrush piping one mellow des-
cant more,
And scent the flowers that blow when the heat
of day is o'er.

Behold the portals open, and o'er the threshold,
now,
There steps a weary one with a pale and furrowed brow;
His count of years is full, his allotted task is
wrought;
He passes to his rest from a place that needs
him not.

In sadness then I ponder how quickly fleets the
hour
Of human strength and action, man's courage
and his power.
I muse while still the woodthrush sings down
the golden day,
And as I look and listen the sadness wears
away.
5

Again the hinges turn, and a youth, departing,
    throws
A look of longing backward, and sorrowfully
    goes;
A blooming maid, unbinding the roses from
    her hair,
Moves mournfully away from amidst the young
    and fair.

Oh glory of our race that so suddenly decays!
Oh crimson flush of morning that darkens as
    we gaze!
Oh breath of summer blossoms that on the
    restless air
Scatters a moment's sweetness and flies we
    know not where!

I grieve for life's bright promise, just shown
    and then withdrawn;
But still the sun shines round me: the evening
    bird sings on,

And I again am soothed, and, beside the ancient gate,
In this soft evening sunlight, I calmly stand
and wait.

Once more the gates are opened; an infant
group go out,
The sweet smile quenched forever, and stilled
the sprightly shout.
Oh frail, frail tree of Life, that upon the greensward strows
Its fair young buds unopened, with every wind
that blows!

So come from every region, so enter, side by
side,
The strong and faint of spirit, the meek and
men of pride.
Steps of earth's great and mighty, between
those pillars gray,
And prints of little feet, mark the dust along
the way.

And some approach the threshold whose looks
    are blank with fear,
And some whose temples brighten with joy in
    drawing near,
As if they saw dear faces, and caught the gra-
    cious eye
Of Him, the Sinless Teacher, who came for us
    to die.

I mark the joy, the terror; yet these, within my
    heart,
Can neither wake the dread nor the longing to
    depart;
And, in the sunshine streaming on quiet wood
    and lea,
I stand and calmly wait till the hinges turn for
    me.

NOT YET.

Oh country, marvel of the earth!
   Oh realm to sudden greatness grown!
The age that gloried in thy birth,
   Shall it behold thee overthrown?
Shall traitors lay that greatness low?
No, land of Hope and Blessing, No!

And we, who wear thy glorious name,
   Shall we, like cravens, stand apart,
When those whom thou hast trusted aim
   The death blow at thy generous heart?
Forth goes the battle cry, and lo!
Hosts rise in harness, shouting, No!

And they who founded, in our land,
    The power that rules from sea to sea,
Bled they in vain, or vainly planned
    To leave their country great and free?
Their sleeping ashes, from below,
Send up the thrilling murmur, No!

Knit they the gentle ties which long
    These sister States were proud to wear,
And forged the kindly links so strong
    For idle hands in sport to tear?
For scornful hands aside to throw?
No, by our fathers' memory, No!

Our humming marts, our iron ways,
    Our wind-tossed woods on mountain-crest,
The hoarse Atlantic, with its bays,
    The calm, broad Ocean of the West,
And Mississippi's torrent-flow,
And loud Niagara, answer, No!

Not yet the hour is nigh when they
   Who deep in Eld's dim twilight sit,
Earth's ancient kings, shall rise and say,
   "Proud country, welcome to the pit!
So soon art thou, like us, brought low!"
No, sullen group of shadows, No!

For now, behold, the arm that gave
   The victory in our fathers day,
Strong, as of old, to guard and save—
   That mighty arm which none can stay—
On clouds above and fields below,
Writes, in men's sight, the answer, No!

July, 1861.

OUR COUNTRY'S CALL.

Lay down the axe; fling by the spade;
  Leave in its track the toiling plough;
The rifle and the bayonet blade
  For arms like yours were fitter now;
And let the hands that ply the pen
  Quit the light task, and learn to wield
The horseman's crooked brand, and rein
  The charger on the battle field.

Our country calls; away! away!
  To where the blood-stream blots the green.
Strike to defend the gentlest sway
  That Time in all his course has seen.

See, from a thousand coverts—see,
    Spring the armed foes that haunt her track;
They rush to smite her down, and we
    Must beat the banded traitors back.

Ho! sturdy as the oaks ye cleave,
    And moved as soon to fear and flight,
Men of the glade and forest! leave
    Your woodcraft for the field of fight.
The arms that wield the axe must pour
    An iron tempest on the foe;
His serried ranks shall reel before
    The arm that lays the panther low.

And ye, who breast the mountain storm
    By grassy steep or highland lake,
Come, for the land ye love, to form
    A bulwark that no foe can break.
Stand, like your own gray cliffs that mock
    The whirlwind, stand in her defence;
The blast as soon shall move the rock
    As rushing squadrons bear ye thence.
5*

And ye, whose homes are by her grand
    Swift rivers, rising far away,
Come from the depth of her green land,
    As mighty in your march as they ;
As terrible as when the rains
    Have swelled them over bank and bourne,
With sudden floods to drown the plains
    And sweep along the woods uptorn.

And ye, who throng, beside the deep,
    Her ports and hamlets of the strand,
In number like the waves that leap
    On his long murmuring marge of sand,
Come, like that deep, when, o'er his brim,
    He rises, all his floods to pour,
And flings the proudest barks that swim,
    A helpless wreck, against his shore.

Few, few were they whose swords of old
    Won the fair land in which we dwell ;
But we are many, we who hold
    The grim resolve to guard it well.

Strike, for that broad and goodly land,
   Blow after blow, till men shall see
That Might and Right move hand in hand,
   And glorious must their triumph be.

September, 1861.

THE CONSTELLATIONS.

Oh, Constellations of the early night
That sparkled brighter as the twilight died,
And made the darkness glorious! I have seen
Your rays grow dim upon the horizon's edge,
And sink behind the mountains. I have seen
The great Orion, with his jewelled belt,
That large-limbed warrior of the skies, go down
Into the gloom. Beside him sank a crowd
Of shining ones. I look in vain to find
The group of sister-stars, which mothers love
To show their wondering babes, the gentle
    Seven.

Along the desert space mine eyes in vain
Seek the resplendent cressets which the Twins
Uplifted in their ever-youthful hands.
The streaming tresses of the Egyptian Queen
Spangle the heavens no more. The Virgin
      trails
No more her glittering garments through the
      blue.
Gone ! all are gone ! and the forsaken Night,
With all her winds, in all her dreary wastes,
Sighs that they shine upon her face no more.
    Now only here and there a little star
Looks forth alone. Ah me ! I know them not,
Those dim successors of the numberless host
That filled the heavenly fields, and flung to
      earth
Their quivering fires. And now the middle
      watch
Betwixt the eve and morn is past, and still
The darkness gains upon the sky, and still
It closes round my way. Shall, then, the night,

Grow starless in her later hours?   Have these
No train of flaming watchers, that shall mark
Their coming and farewell?   Oh Sons of Light!
Have ye then left me ere the dawn of day
To grope along my journey sad and faint?

 Thus I complained, and from the darkness
  round
A voice replied—was it indeed a voice,
Or seeming accents of a waking dream
Heard by the inner ear?   But thus it said:
Oh, Traveller of the Night! thine eyes are dim
With watching; and the mists, that chill the
  vale
Down which thy feet are passing, hide from
  view
The ever-burning stars.   It is thy sight
That is so dark, and not the heavens.   Thine
  eyes,
Were they but clear, would see a fiery host
Above thee; Hercules, with flashing mace,
The Lyre with silver chords, the Swan uppoised

On gleaming wings, the Dolphin gliding on
With glistening scales, and that poetic steed,
With beamy mane, whose hoof struck out from
    earth
The fount of Hippocrene, and many more,
Fair clustered splendors, with whose rays the
    Night
Shall close her march in glory, ere she yield,
To the young Day, the great earth steeped in
    dew.
    So spake the monitor, and I perceived
How vain were my repinings, and my thought
Went backward to the vanished years and all
The good and great who came and passed with
    them,
And knew that ever would the years to come
Bring with them, in their course, the good and
    great,
Lights of the world, though, to my clouded
    sight,
Their rays might seem but dim, or reach me
    not.

THE THIRD OF NOVEMBER, 1861.

SOFTLY breathes the westwind beside the ruddy
  forest,
 Taking leaf by leaf from the branches where
  he flies.
Sweetly streams the sunshine, this third day of
  November,
 Through the golden haze of the quiet autumn
  skies.

Tenderly the season has spared the grassy
  meadows,
 Spared the petted flowers that the old world
  gave the new,

Spared the autumn rose and the garden's group
    of pansies,
  Late-blown dandelions and periwinkles blue.

On my cornice linger the ripe black grapes un-
    gathered ;
  Children fill the groves with the echoes of
    their glee,
Gathering tawny chestnuts, and shouting when
    beside them
  Drops the heavy fruit of the tall black-wal-
    nut tree.

Glorious are the woods in their latest gold and
    crimson,
  Yet our full-leaved willows are in their fresh-
    est green.
Such a kindly autumn, so mercifully dealing
  With the growths of summer, I never yet
    have seen.

Like this kindly season may life's decline come
    o'er me ;
  Past is manhood's summer, the frosty months
    are here ;
Yet be genial airs and a pleasant sunshine left
    me,
  Leaf, and fruit, and blossom, to mark the
    closing year.

Dreary is the time when the flowers of earth
    are withered ;
  Dreary is the time when the woodland leaves
    are cast,
When, upon the hillside, all hardened into
    iron,
  Howling, like a wolf, flies the famished
    northern blast.

Dreary are the years when the eye can look no
    longer
  With delight on nature, or hope on human
    kind ;

Oh may those that whiten my temples, as they
    pass me,
Leave the heart unfrozen, and spare the
    cheerful mind.

THE MOTHER'S HYMN.

LORD, who ordainest for mankind
  Benignant toils and tender cares!
We thank thee for the ties that bind
  The mother to the child she bears.

We thank thee for the hopes that rise,
  Within her heart, as, day by day,
The dawning soul, from those young eyes,
  Looks, with a clearer, steadier ray.

And grateful for the blessing given
  With that dear infant on her knee,
She trains the eye to look to heaven,
  The voice to lisp a prayer to thee.

Such thanks the blessed Mary gave,
   When, from her lap, the Holy Child
Sent from on high to seek and save
   The lost of earth, looked up and smiled.

All-Gracious! grant, to those who bear
   A mother's charge, the strength and light
To lead the steps that own their care
   In ways of Love, and Truth, and Right.

SELLA.

HEAR now a legend of the days of old—
The days when there were goodly marvels yet,
When man to man gave willing faith, and
     loved
A tale the better that 'twas wild and strange.
     Beside a pleasant dwelling ran a brook
Scudding along a narrow channel, paved
With green and yellow pebbles; yet full clear
Its waters were, and colorless and cool,
As fresh from granite rocks.   A maiden oft
Stood at the open window, leaning out,
And listening to the sound the water made,

A sweet, eternal murmur, still the same,
And not the same; and oft, as spring came on,
She gathered violets from its fresh moist bank,
To place within her bower, and when the herbs
Of summer drooped beneath the midday sun,
She sat within the shade of a great rock,
Dreamily listening to the streamlet's song.

    Ripe were the maiden's years; her stature
      showed
Womanly beauty, and her clear, calm eye
Was bright with venturous spirit, yet her face
Was passionless, like those by sculptor graved
For niches in a temple.   Lovers oft
Had wooed her, but she only laughed at love,
And wondered at the silly things they said.
'Twas her delight to wander where wild vines
O'erhang the river's brim, to climb the path
Of woodland streamlet to its mountain springs,
To sit by gleaming wells and mark below'
The image of the rushes on its edge,
And, deep beyond, the trailing clouds that slid

Across the fair blue space.   No little fount
Stole forth from hanging rock, or in the side
Of hollow dell, or under roots of oak,
No rill came trickling, with a stripe of green,
Down the bare hill, that to this maiden's eyes
Was not familiar.   Often did the banks
Of river or of sylvan lakelet hear
The dip of oars with which the maiden rowed
Her shallop, pushing ever from the prow
A crowd of long, light ripples toward the shore.
    Two brothers had the maiden, and she
        thought,
Within herself: " I would I were like them ;
For then I might go forth alone, to trace
The mighty rivers downward to the sea,
And upward to the brooks that, through the
    year,
Prattle to the cool valleys.   I would know
What races drink their waters; how their
        chiefs
Bear rule, and how men worship there, and how

They build, and to what quaint device they
    frame,
Where sea and river meet, their stately ships;
What flowers are in their gardens, and what
    trees
Bear fruit within their orchards; in what garb
Their bowmen meet on holidays, and how
Their maidens bind the waist and braid the
    hair.
Here, on these hills, my father's house o'erlooks
Broad pastures grazed by flocks and herds, but
    there·
I hear they sprinkle the great plains with corn
And watch its springing up, and when the
    green
Is changed to gold, they cut the stems and
    bring
The harvest in, and give the nations bread.
And there they hew the quarry into shafts,
And pile up glorious temples from the rock,
And chisel the rude stones to shapes of men.
   6

All this I pine to see, and would have seen,
But that I am a woman, long ago."
    Thus in her wanderings did the maiden
      dream,
Until, at length, one morn in early spring,
When all the glistening fields lay white with
      frost,
She came half breathless where her mother sat:
"See, mother dear," she said, "what I have
      found,
Upon our rivulet's bank; two slippers, white
As the mid-winter snow, and spangled o'er
With twinkling points, like stars, and on the
      edge
My name is wrought in silver; read, I pray,
Sella, the name thy mother, now in heaven,
Gave at my birth; and sure, they fit my feet!"
"A dainty pair," the prudent matron said,
"But thine they are not. We must lay them by
For those whose careless hands have left them
      here;

Or haply they were placed beside the brook
To be a snare.   I cannot see thy name
Upon the border,—only characters
Of mystic look and dim are there, like signs
Of some strange art; nay, daughter, wear them
    not."
    Then Sella hung the slippers in the porch
Of that broad rustic lodge, and all who passed,
Admired their fair contexture, but none knew
Who left them by the brook And now, at
    length,
May, with her flowers and singing birds, had
    gone,
And on bright streams and into deep wells
    shone
The high, mid-summer sun.   One day, at noon,
Sella was missed from the accustomed meal.
They sought her in her favorite haunts, they
    looked
By the great rock, and far along the stream,
And shouted in the sounding woods her name.

Night came, and forth the sorrowing household
    went
With torches over the wide pasture grounds
To pool and thicket, marsh and briery dell,
And solitary valley far away.
The morning came, and Sella was not found.
The sun climbed high ; they sought her still ;
    the noon,
The hot and silent noon, heard Sella's name,
Uttered with a despairing cry, to wastes
O'er which the eagle hovered.   As the sun
Stooped toward the amber west to bring the
    close
Of that sad second day, and, with red eyes,
The mother sat within her home alone,
Sella was at her side.   A shriek of joy
Broke the sad silence ; glad, warm tears were
    shed,
And words of gladness uttered. "Oh, forgive,"
The maiden said, " that I could e'er forget
Thy wishes for a moment.   I just tried

The slippers on, amazed to see them shaped
So fairly to my feet, when, all at once,
I felt my steps upborne and hurried on
Almost as if with wings. A strange delight,
Blent with a thrill of fear, o'ermastered me,
And, ere I knew, my plashing steps were set
Within the rivulet's pebbly bed, and I
Was rushing down the current. By my side
Tripped one as beautiful as ever looked
From white clouds in a dream ; and, as we ran,
She talked with musical voice and sweetly
　　　laughed ;
Gayly we leaped the crag and swam the pool,
And swept with dimpling eddies round the
　　　rock,
And glided between shady meadow banks.
The streamlet, broadening as we went, became
A swelling river, and we shot along
By stately towns, and under leaning masts
Of gallant barks, nor lingered by the shore
Of blooming gardens ; onward, onward still,

The same strong impulse bore me till, at last,
We entered the great deep, and passed below
His billows, into boundless spaces, lit
With a green sunshine. Here were mighty
     groves
Far down the ocean valleys, and between
Lay what might seem fair meadows, softly
     tinged
With orange and with crimson. Here arose
Tall stems, that, rooted in the depths below,
Swung idly with the motions of the sea ;
And here were shrubberies in whose mazy
     screen
The creatures of the deep made haunt. My
     friend
Named the strange growths, the pretty coral-
     line,
The dulse with crimson leaves, and streaming
     far,
Sea-thong and sea-lace. Here the tangle spread
Its broad, thick fronds, with pleasant bowers
     beneath,

And oft we trod a waste of pearly sands,
Spotted with rosy shells, and thence looked in
At caverns of the sea whose rock-roofed halls
Lay in blue twilight.   As we moved along,
The dwellers of the deep, in mighty herds,
Passed by us, reverently they passed us by,
Long trains of dolphins rolling through the
          brine,
Huge whales, that drew the waters after them,
A torrent stream, and hideous hammer-sharks,
Chasing their prey ; I shuddered as they came ;
Gently they turned aside and gave us room."

    Hereat broke in the mother, " Sella, dear,
This is a dream, the idlest, vainest dream."

    " Nay, mother, nay ; behold this sea-green
          scarf,
Woven of such threads as never human hand
Twined from the distaff.   She who led my way
Through the great waters, bade me wear it
          home,
A token that my tale is true.   ' And keep,'

She said, 'the slippers thou hast found, for
     thou,
When shod with them, shalt be like one of us,
With power to walk at will the ocean floor,
Among its monstrous creatures unafraid,
And feel no longing for the air of heaven
To fill thy lungs, and send the warm, red blood
Along thy veins. But thou shalt pass the hours
In dances with the sea-nymphs, or go forth,
To look into the mysteries of the abyss
Where never plummet reached. And thou
     shalt sleep
Thy weariness away on downy banks
Of sea-moss, where the pulses of the tide
Shall gently lift thy hair, or thou shalt float
On the soft currents that go forth and wind
From isle to isle, and wander through the sea.'
   " So spake my fellow-voyager, her words
Sounding like wavelets on a summer shore,
And then we stopped beside a hanging rock
With a smooth beach of white sands at its foot,

Where three fair creatures like herself were set
At their sea-banquet, crisp and juicy stalks,
Culled from the ocean's meadows, and the
    sweet
Midrib of pleasant leaves, and golden fruits,
Dropped from the trees that edge the southern
    isles,
And gathered on the waves. Kindly they
    prayed
That I would share their meal, and I partook
With eager appetite, for long had been
My journey, and I left the spot refreshed.
    " And then we wandered off amid the groves
Of coral loftier than the growths of earth ;
The mightiest cedar lifts no trunk like theirs,
So huge, so high, toward heaven, nor over-
    hangs
Alleys and bowers so dim. We moved between
Pinnacles of black rock, which, from beneath,
Molten by inner fires, so said my guide,
Gushed long ago into the hissing brine,
    6*

That quenched and hardened them, and now
    they stand
Motionless in the currents of the sea
That part and flow around them. As we went,
We looked into the hollows of the abyss,
To which the never-resting waters sweep
The skeletons of sharks, the long white spines
Of narwhale and of dolphin, bones of men
Shipwrecked, and mighty ribs of foundered
    barks.
Down the blue pits we looked, and hastened
    on.
    " But beautiful the fountains of the sea
Sprang upward from its bed ; the silvery jets
Shot branching far into the azure brine,
And where they mingled with it, the great
    deep
Quivered and shook, as shakes the glimmering
    air
Above a furnace. So we wandered through
The mighty world of waters, till, at length

I wearied of its wonders, and my heart
Began to yearn for my dear mountain home.
I prayed my gentle guide to lead me back
To the upper air. 'A glorious realm,' I said,
'Is this thou openest to me; but I stray
Bewildered in its vastness; these strange sights
And this strange light oppress me. I must see
The faces that I love, or I shall die.'

    " She took my hand, and, darting through the waves,
Brought me to where the stream, by which we came,
Rushed into the main ocean. Then began
A slower journey upward. Wearily
We breasted the strong current, climbing through
The rapids tossing high their foam. The night
Came down, and, in the clear depth of a pool,
Edged with o'erhanging rock, we took our rest
Till morning; and I slept, and dreamed of home
And thee. A pleasant sight the morning showed;

The green fields of this upper world, the herds
That grazed the bank, the light on the red
    clouds,
The trees, with all their host of trembling leaves,
Lifting and lowering to the restless wind
Their branches. As I woke I saw them all
From the clear stream; yet strangely was my
    heart
Parted between the watery world and this,
And as we journeyed upward, oft I thought
Of marvels I had seen, and stopped and turned,
And lingered, till I thought of thee again;
And then again I turned and clambered up
The rivulet's murmuring path, until we came
Beside this cottage door. There tenderly
My fair conductor kissed me, and I saw
Her face no more. I took the slippers off.
Oh! with what deep delight my lungs drew in
The air of heaven again, and with what joy
I felt my blood bound with its former glow;
And now I never leave thy side again."

So spoke the maiden Sella, with large tears
Standing in her mild eyes, and in the porch
Replaced the slippers. Autumn came and
    went;
The winter passed; another summer warmed
The quiet pools; another autumn tinged
The grape with red, yet while it hung un-
    plucked,
The mother ere her time was carried forth
To sleep among the solitary hills.

    A long still sadness settled on that home
Among the mountains. The stern father there
Wept with his children, and grew soft of heart,
And Sella, and the brothers twain, and one
Younger than they, a sister fair and shy,
Strewed the new grave with flowers, and round
    it set
Shrubs that all winter held their lively green.
Time passed; the grief with which their hearts
    were wrung
Waned to a gentle sorrow. Sella, now,

Was often absent from the patriarch's board;
The slippers hung no longer in the porch;
And sometimes after summer nights her couch
Was found unpressed at dawn, and well they
        knew
That she was wandering with the race who
        make
Their dwelling in the waters.   Oft her looks
Fixed on blank space, and oft the ill-suited
        word
Told that her thoughts were far away.   In vain
Her brothers reasoned with her tenderly.
"Oh leave not thus thy kindred;" so they
        prayed;
" Dear Sella, now that she who gave us birth
Is in her grave, oh go not hence, to seek
Companions in that strange cold realm below,
For which God made not us nor thee, but stay
To be the grace and glory of our home."
She looked at them with those mild eyes and
        wept,

But said no word in answer, nor refrained
From those mysterious wanderings that filled
Their loving hearts with a perpetual pain.
    And now the younger sister, fair and shy,
Had grown to early womanhood, and one
Who loved her well had wooed her for his
        bride,
And she had named the wedding day. The
        herd
Had given its fatlings for the marriage feast;
The roadside **garden and** the secret glen
Were rifled of their sweetest flowers to twine
The door posts, and to lie among the locks
Of maids, the wedding guests, and from the
        boughs
Of mountain orchards had the fairest fruit
Been plucked to glisten in the canisters.
    Then, trooping over hill and valley, came
Matron and maid, grave men and smiling
        youths,
Like swallows gathering for their autumn
        flight.

In costumes of that simpler age they came,
That gave the limbs large play, and wrapt the
      form
In easy folds, yet bright with glowing hues
As suited holidays.   All hastened on
To that glad bridal.   There already stood
The priest prepared to say the spousal rite,
And there the harpers in due order sat,
And there the singers.   Sella, midst them all,
Moved strangely and serenely beautiful,
With clear blue eyes, fair locks, and brow and
      cheek
Colorless as the lily of the lakes,
Yet moulded to such shape as artists give
To beings of immortal youth.   Her hands
Had decked her sister for the bridal hour
With chosen flowers, and lawn whose delicate
      threads
Vied with the spider's spinning.   There she
      stood
With such a gentle pleasure in her looks

As might beseem a river-nymph's soft eyes
Gracing a bridal of the race whose flocks
Were pastured on the borders of her stream.
  She smiled, but from that calm sweet face the smile
Was soon to pass away. That very morn
The elder of the brothers, as he stood
Upon the hillside, had beheld the maid,
Emerging from the channel of the brook,
With three fresh water lilies in her hand,
Wring dry her dripping locks, and in a cleft
Of hanging rock, beside a screen of boughs,
Bestow the spangled slippers. None before
Had known where Sella hid them. Then she laid
The light brown tresses smooth, and in them twined
The lily buds, and hastily drew forth
And threw across her shoulders a light robe
Wrought for the bridal, and with bounding steps

Ran toward the lodge.   The youth beheld and
    marked
The spot and slowly followed from afar.
    Now had the marriage rite been said; the
    bride
Stood in the blush that from her burning cheek
Glowed down the alabaster neck, as morn
Crimsons the pearly heaven halfway to the
    west.
At once the harpers struck their chords; a
    gush
Of music broke upon the air; the youths
All started to the dance.   Among them moved
The queenly Sella with a grace that seemed
Caught from the swaying of the summer sea.
The young drew forth the elders to the dance,
Who joined it half abashed, but when they felt
The joyous music tingling in their veins,
They called for quaint old measures, which they
    · trod
As gayly as in youth, and far abroad

Came through the open windows cheerful
    shouts
And bursts of laughter. They who heard the
    sound
Upon the mountain footpaths paused and said,
" A merry wedding." Lovers stole away
That sunny afternoon to bowers that edged
The garden walks, and what was whispered
    there
The lovers of these later times can guess.
    Meanwhile the brothers, when the merry
    din
Was loudest, stole to where the slippers lay,
And took them thence, and followed down the
    brook
To where a little rapid rushed between
Its borders of smooth rock, and dropped them
    in.
The rivulet, as they touched its face, flung up
Its small bright waves like hands, and seemed
    to take
The prize with eagerness and draw it down.

They, gleaming through the waters as they
    went,
And striking with light sound the shining
    stones,
Slid down the stream. The brothers looked
    and watched
And listened with full beating hearts till now
The sight and sound had passed, and silently
And half repentant hastened to the lodge.

    The sun was near his set; the music rang
Within the dwelling still, but the mirth waned;
For groups of guests were sauntering toward
    their homes
Across the fields, and far on hillside paths,
Gleamed the white robes of maidens. Sella
    grew
Weary of the long merriment; she thought
Of her still haunts beneath the soundless sea,
And all unseen withdrew and sought the cleft
Where she had laid the slippers. They were
    gone.

She searched the brookside near, yet found
    them not.
Then her heart sank within her, and she ran
Wildly from place to place, and once again
She searched the secret cleft, and next she
    stooped
And with spread palms felt carefully beneath
The tufted herbs and bushes, and again,
And yet again she searched the rocky cleft.
"Who could have taken them?" That ques-
    tion cleared
The mystery. She remembered suddenly
That when the dance was in its gayest whirl,
Her brothers were not seen, and when, at
    length,
They reappeared, the elder joined the sports
With shouts of boisterous mirth, and from her
    eye
The younger shrank in silence. "Now, I
    know
The guilty ones," she said, and left the spot,

And stood before the youths with such a look
Of anguish and reproach that well they knew
Her thought, and almost wished the deed un-
    done.
    Frankly they owned the charge: "And par-
    don us;
We did it all in love; we could not bear
That the cold world of waters and the strange
Beings that dwell within it should beguile
Our sister from us."   Then they told her all;
How they had seen her stealthily bestow
The slippers in the cleft, and how by stealth
They took them thence and bore them down
    the brook,
And dropped them in, and how the eager waves
Gathered and drew them down: but at that
    word
The maiden shrieked—a broken-hearted shriek—
And all who heard it shuddered and turned
    pale
At the despairing cry, and "They are gone,"

She said, "gone—gone forever. Cruel ones!
'Tis you who shut me out eternally
From that serener world which I had learned
To love so well. Why took ye not my life?
Ye cannot know what ye have done." She
      spake
And hurried to her chamber, and the guests
Who yet had lingered silently withdrew.

    The brothers followed to the maiden's
      bower,
But with a calm demeanor, as they came,
She met them at the door. "The wrong is
      great,"
She said, "that ye have done me, but no power
Have ye to make it less, nor yet to soothe
My sorrow; I shall bear it as I may,
The better for the hours that I have passed
In the calm region of the middle sea.
Go, then. I need you not." They, overawed,
Withdrew from that grave presence. Then her
      tears

Broke forth a flood, as when the August cloud,
Darkening beside the mountain, suddenly
Melts into streams of rain.   That weary night
She paced her chamber, murmuring as she
       walked,
" Oh peaceful region of the middle sea !
Oh azure bowers and grots, in which I loved
To roam and rest !   Am I to long for you,
And think how strangely beautiful ye are,
Yet never see you more ?   And dearer yet,
Ye gentle ones in whose sweet company
I trod the shelly pavements of the deep,
And swam its currents, creatures with calm
       eyes
Looking the tenderest love, and voices soft
As ripple of light waves along the shore,
Uttering the tenderest words !   Oh ! ne'er again
Shall I, in your mild aspects, read the peace
That dwells within, and vainly shall I pine
To hear your sweet low voices.   Haply now
Ye miss me in your deep-sea home, and think

Of me with pity, as of one condemned
To haunt this upper world, with its harsh
    sounds
And glaring lights, its withering heats, its
    frosts,
Cruel and killing, its delirious strifes,
And all its feverish passions, till I die.
    So mourned she the long night, and when
    the morn
Brightened the mountains, from her lattice
    looked
The maiden on a world that was to her
A desolate and dreary waste. That day
She passed in wandering by the brook that oft
Had been her pathway to the sea, and still
Seemed, with its cheerful murmur, to invite
Her footsteps thither. "Well may'st thou re-
    joice,
Fortunate stream!" she said, "and dance along
Thy bed, and make thy course one ceaseless
    strain
    7

Of music, for thou journeyest toward the deep,
To which I shall return no more." The night
Brought her to her lone chamber, and she knelt
And prayed, with many tears, to Him whose
    hand
Touches the wounded heart and it is healed.
With prayer there came new thoughts and new
    desires.
She asked for patience and a deeper love
For those with whom her lot was henceforth
    cast,
And that in acts of mercy she might lose
The sense of her own sorrow. When she rose
A weight was lifted from her heart. She
    sought
Her couch, and slept a long and peaceful sleep.
At morn she woke to a new life. Her days
Henceforth were given to quiet tasks of good
In the great world. Men hearkened to her
    words,
And wondered at their wisdom and obeyed,

And saw how beautiful the law of love
Can make the cares and toils of daily life.
   Still did she love to haunt the springs and
     brooks,
As in her cheerful childhood, and she taught
The skill to pierce the soil and meet the veins
Of clear cold water winding underneath,
And call them forth to daylight. From afar
She bade men bring the rivers on long rows
Of pillared arches to the sultry town,
And on the hot air of the summer fling
The spray of dashing fountains. To relieve
Their weary hands, she showed them how to
     tame
The rushing stream, and make him drive the
     wheel
That whirls the humming millstone and that
     wields
The ponderous sledge. The waters of the
     cloud,
That drench the hillside in the time of rains,

Were gathered at her bidding into pools,
And in the months of drought led forth again,
In glimmering rivulets, to refresh the vales,
Till the sky darkened with returning showers.

    So passed her life, a long and blameless life,
And far and near her name was named with
      love
And reverence. Still she kept, as age came on,
Her stately presence; still her eyes looked
      forth
From under their calm brows as brightly clear
As the transparent wells by which she sat
So oft in childhood. Still she kept her fair
Unwrinkled features, though her locks were
      white.
A hundred times had summer since her birth
Opened the water lily on the lakes,
So old traditions tell, before she died.
A hundred cities mourned her, and her death
Saddened the pastoral valleys. By the brook,
That bickering ran beside the cottage door

Where she was born, they reared her monu-
    ment.
Ere long the current parted and flowed round
The marble base, forming a little isle,
And there the flowers that love the running
    stream,
Iris and orchis, and the cardinal flower,
Crowded and hung caressingly around
The stone engraved with Sella's honored name.

FIFTH BOOK OF HOMER'S ODYSSEY.

TRANSLATED.

AURORA, rising from her couch beside
The famed Tithonus, brought the light of day
To men and to immortals.   Then the gods
Came to their seats in council.   With them
    came
High thundering Jupiter, amongst them all
The mightiest.   Pallas, mindful of the past,
Spoke of Ulysses and his many woes,
Grieved that he still was with the island
    nymph.

" Oh, father Jove, and all ye blessed ones
Who live forever ! let not sceptred king
Henceforth, be gracious, mild, and merciful,
And righteous ; rather be he deaf to prayer,
And prone to deeds of wrong, since no one now
Remembers the divine Ulysses more
Among the people over whom he ruled,
Benignly, like a father.   Still he lies,
Weighed down by many sorrows, in the isle
And dwelling of Calypso, who so long
Constrains his stay.   To his dear native land
Depart he cannot ; ship, arrayed with oars,
And seamen has he none, to bear him o'er
The breast of the broad ocean.   Nay, even now,
Against his well-beloved son a plot
Is laid, to slay him as he journeys home
From Pylos the divine, and from the walls
Of famous Sparta, whither he had gone
To gather tidings of his father's fate."

Then answered her the ruler of the storms :
" My child, what words are these that pass thy
   lips ?

Was not thy long-determined counsel this,
That, in good time, Ulysses should return,
To be avenged?   Guide, then, Telemachus,
Wisely, for so thou canst, that, all unharmed,
He reach his native land, and, in their barks,
Homeward the suitor-train retrace their way."
   He spoke, and turned to Hermes, his dear
   son :
" Hermes, for thou, in this, my messenger
Art, as in all things, to the bright-haired
   nymph
Make known my steadfast purpose, the return
Of suffering Ulysses.   Neither gods
Nor men shall guide his voyage.   On a raft,
Made firm with bands, he shall depart and
   reach,
After long hardships, on the twentieth day,
The fertile shore of Scheria, on whose isle
Dwell the Pheacians, kinsmen of the gods.
They like a god shall honor him, and thence
Send him to his loved country in a ship,

With ample gifts of brass and gold, and store
Of raiment—wealth like which he ne'er had
    brought
From conquered Ilion, had he reached his home
Safely, with all his portion of the spoil.
So is it preordained, that he behold
His friends again, and stand once more within
His high-roofed palace, on his native soil."
    He spake; the herald Argicide obeyed,
And hastily beneath his feet he bound
The fair, ambrosial, golden sandals, worn
To bear him over ocean like the wind,
And o'er the boundless land. His wand he
    took,
Wherewith he softly seals the eyes of men,
And opens them at will from sleep. With this
In hand, the mighty Argos-queller flew,
And lighting on Pieria, from the sky
Plunged downward to the deep, and skimmed
    its face
Like hovering sea-mew, that on the broad gulfs

7*

Of the unfruitful ocean seeks her prey,
And often dips her pinions in the brine,
So Hermes flew along the waste of waves.

But when he reached that island, far away,
Forth from the dark blue ocean-swell he
    stepped
Upon the sea-beach, walking till he came
To the vast cave in which the bright-haired
    nymph
Made her abode. He found the nymph within.
A fire blazed brightly on the hearth, and far
Was wafted o'er the isle the fragrant smoke
Of cloven cedar, burning in the flame,
And cypress wood. Meanwhile, in her recess,
She sweetly sang, as busily she threw
The golden shuttle through the web she wove.
And all about the grotto alders grew,
And poplars, and sweet-smelling cypresses,
In a green forest, high among whose boughs
Birds of broad wing, wood-owls and falcons,
    built

Their nests, and crows, with voices sounding
    far,
All haunting for their food the ocean side.
A vine, with downy leaves and clustering
    grapes,
Crept over all the cavern rock.   Four springs
Poured forth their glittering waters in a row,
And here and there went wandering side by
    side.
Around were meadows of soft green, o'ergrown
With violets and parsley.   'Twas a spot
Where even an Immortal might, awhile,
Linger, and gaze with wonder and delight.
The herald Argos-queller stood, and saw,
And marvelled ; but as soon as he had viewed
The wonders of the place, he turned his steps,
Entering the broad-roofed cave.   Calypso there,
The glorious goddess, saw him as he came,
And knew him, for the ever-living gods
Are to each other known, though one may
    dwell

Far from the rest.   Ulysses, large of heart,
Was not within.   Apart, upon the shore,
He sat and sorrowed, where he oft, in tears
And sighs and vain repinings, passed the
    hours,
Gazing with wet eyes on the barren deep.
Now, placing Hermes on a shining seat
Of state, Calypso, glorious goddess, said,
    " Thou of the golden wand, revered and
        loved,
What, Hermes, brings thee hither ?   Passing
        few
Have been thy visits.   Make thy pleasure
        known,
My heart enjoins me to obey, if aught
That thou commandest be within my power,
But first accept the offerings due a guest."
    The goddess, speaking thus, before him
        placed
A table where the heaped ambrosia lay,
And mingled the red nectar.   Ate and drank

The herald Argos-queller, and, refreshed,
Answered the nymph, and made his message
        known:
    " Art thou a goddess, and dost ask of me,
A god, why came I hither?   Yet, since thou
Requirest, I will truly tell the cause.
I came unwillingly at Jove's command,
For who, of choice, would traverse the wide
        waste
Of the salt ocean, with no city near,
Where men adore the gods with solemn rites
And chosen hecatombs.   No god has power
To elude or to resist the purposes
Of ægis-bearing Jove.   With thee abides,
He bids me say, the most unhappy man
Of all who round the city of Priam waged
The battle through nine years, and, in the
        tenth,
Laying it waste, departed for their homes.
But, in their voyage, they provoked the wrath
Of Pallas, who called up the furious winds

And angry waves against them. By his side
Sank all his gallant comrades in the deep.
Him did the winds and waves drive hither.
    Him
Jove bids thee send away with speed, for here
He must not perish, far from all he loves.
So is it preordained that he behold
His friends again, and stand once more within
His high-roofed palace, on his native soil."

    He spoke, Calypso, glorious goddess, heard,
And shuddered, and with wingèd words re-
    plied :
    " Ye are unjust, ye gods, and, envious far
Beyond all other beings, cannot bear
That ever goddess openly should make
A mortal man her consort. Thus it was
When once Aurora, rosy-fingered, took
Orion for her husband ; ye were stung,
Amid your blissful lives, with envious hate,
Till chaste Diana, of the golden throne,
Smote him with silent arrows from her bow,

And slew him in Ortygia. Thus, again,
When bright-haired Ceres, swayed by her own
    heart,
In fields which bore three yearly harvests, met
Iasion as a lover, this was known
Ere long to Jupiter, who flung from high
A flaming thunderbolt, and laid him dead.
And now ye envy me, that with me dwells
A mortal man. I saved him, as he clung,
Alone, upon his floating keel, for Jove
Had cloven, with a bolt of fire, from heaven,
His galley in the midst of the black sea,
And all his gallant comrades perished there.
Him kindly I received; I cherished him,
And promised him a life that ne'er should know
Decay or death. But, since no god has power
To elude or to withstand the purposes
Of ægis-bearing Jove, let him depart,
If so the sovereign moves him and commands,
Over the barren deep. I send him not;
For neither ship arrayed with oars have I,

Nor seamen, o'er the boundless waste of waves
To bear him hence.   My counsel I will give,
And nothing will I hide that he should know,
To place him safely on his native shore."
　　The herald Argos-queller answered her :
"Dismiss him thus, and bear in mind the
　　　　wrath
Of Jove, lest it be kindled against thee."
　　Thus having said, the mighty Argicide
Departed, and the nymph, who now had heard
The doom of Jove, sought the great-hearted
　　　　man,
Ulysses.   Him she found beside the deep,
Seated alone, with eyes from which the tears
Were never dried, for now no more the nymph
Delighted him ; he wasted his sweet life
In yearning for his home.   Night after night
He slept constrained within the hollow cave,
The unwilling by the fond, and, day by day,
He sat upon the rocks that edged the shore,
And in continual weeping and in sighs

And vain repinings, wore the hours away,
Gazing through tears upon the barren deep.
The glorious goddess stood by him and spoke :
    " Unhappy ! sit no longer sorrowing here,
Nor waste life thus.   Lo ! I most willingly
Dismiss thee hence.   Rise, hew down trees,
        and bind
Their trunks, with brazen clamps, into a raft,
And fasten planks above, a lofty floor,
That it may bear thee o'er the dark blue deep.
Bread will I put on board, water, and wine,
Red wine, that cheers the heart, and wrap thee
        well
In garments, and send after thee the wind,
That safely thou attain thy native shore ;
If so the gods permit thee, who abide
In the broad heaven above, and better know
By far than I, and far more wisely judge."
    Ulysses, the great sufferer, as she spoke,
Shuddered, and thus with wingèd words re-
        plied.:

"Some other purpose than to send me home
Is in thy heart, oh goddess, bidding me '
To cross this frightful sea upon a raft,
The perilous sea, where never even ships
Pass with their rapid keels, though Jove bestow
The wind that glads the seaman. Nay, I climb
No raft, against thy wish, unless thou swear
The great oath of the gods, that thou, in this,
Dost meditate no other harm to me."

    He   spake; Calypso, glorious goddess,
        smiled,
And smoothed his forehead with her hand, and
        said :
    "Perverse! and slow to see where guile is
        not!
How could thy heart permit thee thus to speak?
Now bear me witness, Earth, and ye broad
        Heavens
Above us, and ye waters of the Styx
That flow beneath us, mightiest oath of all,
And most revered by all the blessed gods,

That I design no other harm to thee ;
But that I plan for thee and counsel thee
What I would do were I in need like thine.
I bear a juster mind ; my bosom holds
A pitying heart, and not a heart of steel."
    Thus having said, the glorious goddess
      moved
Away with hasty steps, and where she trod
He followed, till they reached the vaulted cave,
The goddess and the hero.   There he took
The seat whence Hermes had just risen.   The
      nymph
Brought forth whatever mortals eat and drink
To set before him.   She, right opposite
To that of great Ulysses, took her seat.
Ambrosia there her maidens laid, and there
Poured nectar.   Both put forth their hands,
      and took
The ready viands, till at length the calls
Of hunger and of thirst were satisfied ;
Calypso, glorious goddess, then began :

" Son of Laertes, man of many wiles,
High-born Ulysses! Thus wilt thou depart
Home to thy native country? Then farewell;
But, couldst thou know the sufferings Fate or-
    dains
For thee ere yet thou landest on its shore,
Thou wouldst remain to keep this home with
    me,
And be immortal, strong as is thy wish
To see thy wife—a wish that, day by day,
Possesses thee. I cannot deem myself
In form or face less beautiful than she.
For never with immortals can the race
Of mortal dames in form or face compare."
    Ulysses, the sagacious, answered her,
" Bear with me, gracious goddess; well I know
All thou couldst say. The sage Penelope
In feature and in stature comes not nigh
To thee; for she is mortal, deathless thou
And ever young; yet, day by day, I long
To be at home once more, and pine to see

The hour of my return.   Even though some
    god
Smite me on the black ocean, I shall bear
The stroke, for in my bosom dwells a mind
Patient of suffering ; much have I endured,
And much survived, in tempests on the deep,
And in the battle ; let this happen too."
    He spoke ; the sun went down ; the night
      came on,
And now the twain withdrew to a recess
Deep in the vaulted cave, where, side by side,
They took their rest.   But when the child of
    dawn,
Aurora, rosy-fingered, looked abroad,
Ulysses put his vest and mantle on ;
The nymph too, in a robe of silver white,
Ample, and delicate, and beautiful,
Arrayed herself, and round about her loins
Wound a fair golden girdle, drew a veil
Over her head, and planned to send away
Magnanimous Ulysses.   She bestowed

A heavy axe, of steel, and double edged,
Well fitted to the hand, the handle wrought
Of olive wood, firm set, and beautiful.
A polished adze she gave him next, and led
The way to a far corner of the isle,
Where lofty trees, alders and poplars, stood,
And firs that reached the clouds, sapless and dry
Long since, and fitter thus to ride the waves.
Then, having shown where grew the tallest
      trees,
Calypso, glorious goddess, sought her home.
    Trees then he felled, and soon the task was
      done.
Twenty in all he brought to earth, and squared
Their trunks with the sharp steel, and carefully
He smoothed their sides, and wrought them by
      a line.
Calypso, gracious goddess, having brought
Wimbles, he bored the beams, and, fitting them
Together, made them fast with nails and
      clamps.

As when some builder, skilful in his art,
Frames, for a ship of burden, the broad keel,
Such ample breadth Ulysses gave the raft.
Upon the massy beams he reared a deck,
And floored it with long planks from end to
    end.
On this a mast he raised, and to the mast
Fitted a yard ; he shaped a rudder neat,
To guide the raft along her course, and round
With woven work of willow boughs he fenced
Her sides against the dashings of the sea.
Calypso, gracious goddess, brought him store
Of canvas, which he fitly shaped to sails,
And, rigging her with cords, and ropes, and
    stays,
Heaved her with levers into the great deep.
    'Twas the fourth day ; his labors now were
        done,
And, on the fifth, the goddess from her isle
Dismissed him, newly from the bath, arrayed
In garments given by her, that shed perfumes.

A skin of dark red wine she put on board,
A larger one of water, and for food
A basket, stored with viands such as please
The appetite.　A friendly wind and soft
She sent before.　The great Ulysses spread
His canvas joyfully, to catch the breeze,
And sat and guided with nice care the helm,
Gazing with fixed eye on the Pleiades,
Boötes setting late, and the Great Bear,
By others called the Wain, which, wheeling
　　round,
Looks ever toward Orion, and alone
Dips not into the waters of the deep.
For so Calypso, glorious goddess, bade
That, on his ocean journey, he should keep
That constellation ever on his left.
Now seventeen days were in the voyage past,
And on the eighteenth shadowy heights ap-
　　peared,
The nearest point of the Pheacian land,
Lying on the dark ocean like a shield.

But mighty Neptune, coming from among
The Ethiopians, saw him.   Far away
He saw, from mountain heights of Solyma,
The voyager, and burned with fiercer wrath,
And shook his head, and said within himself:
   "Strange! now I see the gods have new
     designs
For this Ulysses, formed while I was yet
In Ethiopia.   He draws near the land
Of the Pheacians, where it is decreed
He shall o'erpass the boundary of his woes;
But first, I think, he will have much to bear."
   He spoke, and round about him called the
     clouds
And roused the ocean, wielding in his hand
The trident, summoned all the hurricanes
Of all the winds, and covered earth and sky
At once with mists, while from above, the night
Fell suddenly.   The east wind and the south
Rushed forth at once, with the strong-blowing
     west,

8

And the clear north rolled up his mighty waves.
Ulysses trembled in his knees and heart,
And thus to his great soul, lamenting, said:

"What will become of me? unhappy man!
I fear that all the goddess said was true,
Foretelling what disasters should o'ertake
My voyage, ere I reach my native land.
Now are her words fulfilled.   How Jupiter
Wraps the great heaven in clouds and stirs the
        deep
To tumult!   Wilder grow the hurricanes
Of all the winds, and now my fate is sure.
Thrice happy, four times happy they, who fell
On Troy's wide field, warring for Atreus' sons.
Oh, had I met my fate and perished there,
That very day on which the Trojan host,
Around the dead Achilles, hurled at me
Their brazen javelins; I had then received
Due burial and great glory with the Greeks;
Now must I die a miserable death."

As thus he spoke, upon him, from on high,

A huge and frightful billow broke ; it whirled
The raft around, and far from it he fell.
His hands let go the rudder ; a fierce rush
Of all the winds together snapped in twain
The mast ; far off the yard and canvas flew
Into the deep ; the billow held him long
Beneath the waters, and he strove in vain
Quickly to rise to air from that huge swell
Of ocean, for the garments weighed him down
Which fair Calypso gave him.   But, at length,
Emerging, he rejected from his throat
The   bitter   brine   that   down   his   forehead
    streamed.
Even then, though hopeless with dismay, his
    thought
Was on the raft, and, struggling through the
    waves,
He seized it, sprang on board, and seated there
Escaped the threatened death.   Still to and fro
The rolling billows drove it.   As the wind
In autumn sweeps the thistles o'er the field,

Clinging together, so the blasts of heaven
Hither and thither drove it o'er the sea.
And now the south wind flung it to the north
To buffet; now the east wind to the west.

   Ino Leucothea saw him clinging there,
The delicate-footed child of Cadmus, once
A mortal, speaking with a mortal voice,
Though now, within the ocean-gulfs, she shares
The honors of the gods.   With pity she
Beheld Ulysses struggling thus distressed,
And, rising from the abyss below, in form
A cormorant, the sea-nymph took her perch
On the well-banded raft, and thus she said:
   " Ah, luckless man, how hast thou angered
     thus
Earth-shaking Neptune, that he visits thee
With these disasters?   Yet he cannot take,
Although he seek it earnestly, thy life.
Now do my bidding, for thou seemest wise.
Laying aside thy garments, let the raft
Drift with the winds, while thou, by strength
     of arm,

Makest thy way in swimming to the land
Of the Pheacians, where thy safety lies.
Receive this veil and bind its heavenly woof
Beneath thy breast, and have no further fear
Of hardship or of danger.   But, as soon
As thou shalt touch the island, take it off,
And turn away thy face, and fling it far
From where thou standest, into the black deep."

The goddess gave the veil as thus she spoke,
And to the tossing deep went down, in form
A cormorant; the black wave covered her.
But still Ulysses, mighty sufferer,
Pondered, and thus to his great soul he said :

" Ah me ! perhaps some god is planning
    here
Some other fraud against me, bidding me
Forsake my raft.   I will not yet obey,
For still far off I see the land in which
'Tis said my refuge lies.   This will I do,
For this seems wisest.   While the fastenings last
That hold these timbers, I will keep my place

And bide the tempest here. But when the
    waves
Shall dash my raft in pieces, I will swim,
For nothing better will remain to do."
    As he revolved this purpose in his mind,
Earth-shaking Neptune sent a mighty wave,
Horrid, and huge, and high, and where he sat
It smote him. As a violent wind uplifts
The dry chaff heaped upon a threshing floor,
And sends it scattered through the air abroad,
So did that wave fling loose the ponderous
    beams.
To one of these, Ulysses, clinging fast,
Bestrode it, like a horseman on his steed ;
And now he took the garments off, bestowed
By fair Calypso, binding round his breast
The veil, and forward plunged into the deep,
With palms outspread, prepared to swim.
    Meanwhile,
Neptune beheld him, Neptune, mighty king,
And shook his head, and said within himself,

" Go thus, and, laden with mischances,
　　roam
The waters, till thou come among the race
Cherished by Jupiter ; but well I deem
Thou wilt not find thy share of suffering light."
　　Thus having spoke, he urged his coursers on,
With their fair flowing manes, until he came
To Ægæ, where his glorious palace stands.
　　But Pallas, child of Jove, had other
　　　thoughts.
She stayed the course of every wind beside,
And bade them rest, and lulled them into
　　sleep,
But summoned the swift north to break the
　　waves,
That so Ulysses, the high-born, escaped
From death and from the fates, might be the
　　guest
Of the Pheacians, men who love the sea.
　　Two days and nights, among the mighty
　　　waves

He floated, oft his heart foreboding death,
But when the bright-haired Eos had fulfilled
The third day's course, and all the winds were
        laid,
And calm was on the watery waste, he saw
That land was near, as, lifted on the crest
Of a huge swell, he looked with sharpened
        sight ;
And as a father's life preserved makes glad
His children's heart, when long-time he has
        lain
Sick, wrung with pain, and wasting by the
        power
Of some malignant genius, till, at length,
The gracious gods bestow a welcome cure ;
So welcome to Ulysses was the sight
Of woods and fields. By swimming on he
        thought
To climb and tread the shore, but when he drew
So near that one who shouted could be heard
From land, the sound of ocean on the rocks

Came to his ear, for there huge breakers roared
And spouted fearfully, and all around
Was covered with the sea-foam.   Haven here
Was none for ships, nor sheltering creek, but
    shores
Beetling from high, and crags and walls of rock.
Ulysses trembled both in knees and heart,
And thus, to his great soul, lamenting, said :
    "Now woe is me! as soon as Jove has
      shown
What I had little hoped to see, the land,
And I through all these waves have ploughed
    my way,
I find no issue from the hoary deep.
For sharp rocks border it, and all around
Roar the wild surges ; slippery cliffs arise
Close to deep gulfs, and footing there is none,
Where I might plant my steps and thus escape.
All effort now were fruitless to resist
The mighty billow hurrying me away
To dash me on the pointed rocks.   If yet
    8*

I strive, by swimming further, to descry
Some sloping shore or harbor of the isle,
I fear the tempest, lest it hurl me back,
Heavily groaning, to the fishy deep.
Or huge sea monster, from the multitude
Which sovereign Amphitrite feeds, be sent
Against me by some god, for well I know
The power who shakes the shores is wroth with
        me."
    While he revolved these doubts within his
        mind
A huge wave hurled him toward the rugged
        coast.
Then had his limbs been flayed, and all his
        bones
Broken at once, had not the blue-eyed maid,
Minerva, prompted him. Borne toward the rock,
He clutched it instantly, with both his hands,
And, panting, clung, till that huge wave rolled
        by,
And so escaped its fury. Back it came,

And smote him once again, and flung him far
Seaward.   As to the claws of polypus,
Plucked from its bed, the pebbles thickly cling,
So flakes of skin, from off his powerful hands,
Were left upon the rock.   The mighty surge
O'erwhelmed him; he had perished ere his
       time,
Hapless Ulysses, but the blue-eyed maid
Pallas, informed his mind with wisdom.
       Straight
Emerging from the wave that shoreward rolled,
He swam along the coast and eyed it well,
In hope of sloping beach or sheltered creek.
But when, in swimming, he had reached the
       mouth
Of a soft-flowing river, here appeared
The spot he wished for, smooth, without a rock,
And here was shelter from the wind.   He felt
The current's flow, and thus devoutly prayed:

    " Hear me, oh sovereign power, whoe'er
       thou art!

To thee, the long desired, I come.   I seek
Escape from Neptune's threatenings on the sea.
The deathless gods respect the prayer of him
Who looks to them for help, a fugitive,
As I am now, when to thy stream I come,
And to thy knees, from many a hardship past,
Oh thou that here art ruler, I declare
Myself thy suppliant ; be thou merciful."
    He spoke ; the river stayed his current, checked
The billows, smoothed them to a calm, and gave
The swimmer a safe landing at his mouth.
Then dropped his knees and sinewy arms, at once
Unstrung, for faint with struggling was his heart.
His body was all swoln ; the brine gushed forth
From mouth and nostrils ; all unnerved he lay,
Breathless and speechless ; utter weariness

O'ermastered him.　But when he breathed
　　again,
And his flown senses had returned, he loosed
The veil that Ino gave him from his breast,
And to the salt flood cast it.　A great wave
Bore it far down the stream; the goddess there
In her own hands received it.　He, meanwhile,
Withdrawing from the brink, lay down among
The reeds, and kissed the harvest-bearing earth,
And thus to his great soul, lamenting, said:

　　" Ah me! what must I suffer more! what
　　yet
Will happen to me?　If, by the river's side,
I pass the unfriendly watches of the night,
The cruel cold and dews that steep the bank
May, in this weakness, end me utterly
For chilly blows the river air at dawn.
But should I climb this hill, to sleep within
The shadowy wood, among thick shrubs, if cold
And weariness allow me, then I fear,
That, while the pleasant slumbers o'er me steal,
· I may become the prey of savage beasts."

Yet, as he longer pondered this seemed
    best.
He rose and sought the wood, and found it near
The water, on a height, o'erlooking far
The region round. Between two shrubs, that
    sprung
Both from one spot, he entered,—olive trees,
One wild, one fruitful. The damp-blowing
    wind
Ne'er pierced their covert ; never blazing sun
Darted his beams within, nor pelting shower
Beat through, so closely intertwined they grew.
Here entering, Ulysses heaped a bed
Of leaves with his own hands ; he made it
    broad
And high, for thick the leaves had fallen
    around.
Two men and three, in that abundant store,
Might bide the winter storm, though keen the
    cold.
Ulysses, the great sufferer, on his couch

Looked and rejoiced, and placed himself with-
    in,
And heaped the leaves high o'er him and
    around.
    As one who, dwelling in the distant fields,
Without a neighbor near him, hides a brand
In the dark ashes, keeping carefully
The seeds of fire alive, lest he, perforce,
To light his hearth must bring them from afar;
So did Ulysses, in that pile of leaves,
Bury himself, while Pallas o'er his eyes
Poured sleep and closed his lids, that he might
    take,
After his painful toils, the fitting rest.

Revised November 15, 1862.

THE LITTLE PEOPLE OF THE SNOW.

Alice.—One of your old world stories, Uncle
    John,
Such as you tell us by the winter fire,
Till we all wonder it has grown so late.
    Uncle John.—The story of the witch that
    ground to death
Two children in her mill, or will you have
The tale of Goody Cutpurse?
    Alice.—   Nay now, nay;
Those stories are too childish, Uncle John,
Too childish even for little Willy here,
And I am older, two good years, than he;

No, let us have a tale of elves that ride,
By night, with jingling reins, or gnomes of the
    mine,
Or water-fairies, such as you know how
To spin, till Willy's eyes forget to wink,
And good Aunt Mary, busy as she is,
Lays down her knitting.

    Uncle John.—   Listen to me, then.
'Twas in the olden time, long, long ago,
And long before the great oak at our door
Was yet an acorn, on a mountain's side
Lived, with his wife, a cottager.   They dwelt
Beside a glen and near a dashing brook,
A pleasant spot in spring, where first the wren
Was heard to chatter, and, among the grass,
Flowers opened earliest; but, when winter
    came,
That little brook was fringed with other flow-
    ers,—
White flowers, with crystal leaf and stem, that
    grew

In clear November nights.   And, later still,
That mountain glen was filled with drifted
    snows
From side to side, that one might walk across,
While, many a fathom deep, below, the brook
Sang to itself, and leaped and trotted on
Unfrozen, o'er its pebbles, toward the vale.

    Alice.—A mountain's side, you said; the
        Alps, perhaps,
Or our own Alleghanies.

    Uncle John.—   Not so fast,
My young geographer, for then the Alps,
With their broad pastures, haply were untrod
Of herdsman's foot, and never human voice
Had sounded in the woods that overhang
Our Alleghany's streams.   I think it was
Upon the slopes of the great Caucasus,
Or where the rivulets of Ararat
Seek the Armenian vales.   That mountain rose
So high, that, on its top, the winter snow
Was never melted, and the cottagers

Among the summer blossoms, far below,
Saw its white peaks in August from their door.
   One little maiden, in that cottage home,
Dwelt with her parents, light of heart and limb,
Bright, restless, thoughtless, flitting here and
     there,
Like sunshine on the uneasy ocean waves,
And sometimes she forgot what she was bid,
As Alice does.
    Alice.—   Or Willy, quite as oft.
    Uncle John.—But you are older, Alice, two
    good years,
And should be wiser. Eva was the name
Of this young maiden, now twelve summers
    old.
   Now you must know that, in those early
    times,
When autumn days grew pale, there came a
    troop
Of childlike forms from that cold mountain
    top;

With trailing garments through the air they
    came,
Or walked the ground with girded loins, and
    threw
Spangles of silvery frost upon the grass,
And edged the brook with glistening parapets,
And built it crystal bridges, touched the pool,
And turned its face to glass, or, rising thence,
They shook, from their full laps, the soft, light
    snow,
And buried the great earth, as autumn winds
Bury the forest floor in heaps of leaves.

    A beautiful race were they, with baby brows,
And fair, bright locks, and voices like the sound
Of steps on the crisp snow, in which they
    talked
With man, as friend with friend. A merry
    sight
It was, when, crowding round the traveller,
They smote him with their heaviest snow flakes,
    flung

Needles of frost in handfuls at his cheeks,
And, of the light wreaths of his smoking breath,
Wove a white fringe for his brown beard, and
     laughed
Their slender laugh to see him wink and grin
And make grim faces as he floundered on.
    But, when the spring came on, what terror
    reigned
Among these Little People of the Snow!
To them the sun's warm beams were shafts of
    fire,
And the soft south wind was the wind of death.
Away they flew, all with a pretty scowl
Upon their childish faces, to the north,
Or scampered upward to the mountain's top,
And there defied their enemy, the Spring;
Skipping and dancing on the frozen peaks,
And moulding little snow-balls in their palms,
And rolling them, to crush her flowers below,
Down the steep snow-fields.
    Alice.—   That, too, must have been
A merry sight to look at.

Uncle John.—   You are right,
But I must speak of graver matters now.

  Mid-winter was the time, and Eva stood,
Within the cottage, all prepared to dare
The outer cold, with ample furry robe
Close belted round her waist, and boots of fur,
And a broad kerchief, which her mother's
  hand
Had closely drawn about her ruddy cheek.
"Now, stay not long abroad," said the good
  dame,
"For sharp is the outer air, and, mark me well,
Go not upon the snow beyond the spot
Where the great linden bounds the neighboring
  field."

  The little maiden promised, and went forth,
And climbed the rounded snow-swells firm with
  frost
Beneath her feet, and slid, with balancing arms,
Into the hollows.   Once, as up a drift
She slowly rose, before her, in the way,

She saw a little creature lily-cheeked,
With flowing flaxen locks, and faint blue eyes,
That gleamed like ice, and robe that only
  seemed
Of a more shadowy whiteness than her cheek.
On a smooth bank she sat.

    Alice.—   She must have been
One of your Little People of the Snow.

    Uncle John.—She was so, and, as Eva now
  drew near,
The tiny creature bounded from her seat;
" And come," she said, " my pretty friend; to-
  day
We will be playmates. I have watched thee
  long,
And seen how well thou lov'st to walk these
  drifts,
And scoop their fair sides into little cells,
And carve them with quaint figures, huge-
  limbed men,
Lions, and griffins. We will have, to-day,

A merry ramble over these bright fields,
And thou shalt see what thou hast never seen."
    On went the pair, until they reached the
      bound
Where the great linden stood, set deep in snow,
Up to the lower branches.   " Here we stop,"
Said Eva, " for my mother has my word
That I will go no further than this' tree."
Then the snow-maiden laughed ; " And what is
      this ?
This fear of the pure snow, the innocent snow,
That never harmed aught living ? Thou may'st
      roam
For leagues beyond this garden, and return
In safety ; here the grim wolf never prowls,
And here the eagle of our mountain crags
Preys not in winter.   I will show the way
And bring thee safely home.   Thy mother,
      sure,
Counselled thee thus because thou hadst no
      guide."

By such smooth words was Eva won to
    break
Her promise, and went on with her new friend,
Over the glistening snow and down a bank
Where a white shelf, wrought by the eddying
    wind,
Like to a billow's crest in the great sea,
Curtained an opening. "Look, we enter here."
And straight, beneath the fair o'erhanging
    fold,
Entered the little pair that hill of snow,
Walking along a passage with white walls,
And a white vault above where snow-stars
    shed
A wintry twilight. Eva moved in awe,
And held her peace, but the snow-maiden
    smiled,
And talked and tripped along, as, down the
    way,
Deeper they went into that mountainous
    drift.

9

And now the white walls widened, and the
    vault
Swelled upward, like some vast cathedral dome,
Such as the Florentine, who bore the name
Of heaven's most potent angel, reared, long
    since,
Or the unknown builder of that wondrous fane,
The glory of Burgos. Here a garden lay,
In which the Little People of the Snow
Were wont to take their pastime when their
    tasks
Upon the mountain's side and in the clouds
Were ended. Here they taught the silent frost
To mock, in stem and spray, and leaf and flow-
    er,
The growths of summer. Here the palm up-
    reared
Its white columnar trunk and spotless sheaf
Of plume-like leaves; here cedars, huge as
    those
Of Lebanon, stretched far their level boughs,

Yet pale and shadowless; the sturdy oak
Stood, with its huge gnarled roots of seeming
    strength,
Fast anchored in the glistening bank; light
    sprays
Of myrtle, roses in their bud and bloom,
Drooped by the winding walks; yet all seemed
    wrought
Of stainless alabaster; up the trees
Ran the lithe jessamine, with stalk and leaf
Colorless as her flowers.   "Go softly on,"
Said the snow maiden; "touch not, with thy
    hand,
The frail creation round thee, and beware
To sweep it with thy skirts.   Now look above.
How sumptuously these bowers are lighted up
With shifting gleams that softly come and go.
These are the northern lights, such as thou
    seest
In the midwinter nights, cold, wandering
    flames,

That float, with our processions, through the
    air ;
And here, within our winter palaces,
Mimic the glorious daybreak." Then she told
How, when the wind, in the long winter nights,
Swept the light snows into the hollow dell,
She and her comrades guided to its place
Each wandering flake, and piled them quaintly
    up,
In shapely colonnade and glistening arch,
With shadowy aisles between, or bade them
    grow,
Beneath their little hands, to bowery walks
In gardens such as these, and, o'er them all,
Built the broad roof. "But thou hast yet to
    see
A fairer sight," she said, and led the way
To where a window of pellucid ice
Stood in the wall of snow, beside their path.
"Look, but thou mayst not enter." Eva
    looked,

And lo! a glorious hall, from whose high vault
Stripes of soft light, ruddy, and delicate green,
And tender blue, flowed downward to the floor
And far around, as if the aerial hosts,
That march on high by night, with beamy
      spears,
And streaming banners, to that place had
      brought
Their radiant flags to grace a festival.
      And in that hall a joyous multitude
Of those by whom its glistening walls were
      reared,
Whirled in a merry dance to silvery sounds,
That rang from cymbals of transparent ice,
And ice-cups, quivering to the skilful touch
Of little fingers. Round and round they flew,
As when, in spring, about a chimney top,
A cloud of twittering swallows, just returned,
Wheel round and round, and turn and wheel
      again,
Unwinding their swift track. So rapidly

Flowed the meandering stream of that fair
    dance,
Beneath that dome of light. Bright eyes that
    looked
From under lily brows, and gauzy scarfs
Sparkling like snow-wreaths in the early sun,
Shot by the window in their mazy whirl.
And there stood Eva, wondering at the sight
Of those bright revellers and that graceful
    sweep
Of motion as they passed her ;—long she gazed,
And listened long to the sweet sounds that
    thrilled
The frosty air, till now the encroaching cold
Recalled her to herself. "Too long, too long
I linger here," she said, and then she sprang
Into the path, and with a hurried step
Followed it upward. Ever by her side
Her little guide kept pace. As on they went
Eva bemoaned her fault; "What must they
    think—

The dear ones in the cottage, while so long,
Hour after hour, I stay without?   I know
That they will seek me far and near, and weep
To find me not.   How could I, wickedly
Neglect the charge they gave me?"   As she
      spoke,
The hot tears started to her eyes; she knelt
In the mid path.   "Father! forgive this sin;
Forgive myself I cannot"—thus she prayed,
And rose and hastened onward.   When, at
      last,
They reached the outer air, the clear north
      breathed
A bitter cold, from which she shrank with
      dread,
But the snow-maiden bounded as she felt
The cutting blast, and uttered shouts of joy,
And skipped, with boundless glee, from drift to
      drift,
And danced round Eva, as she labored up
The mounds of snow,   "Ah me! I feel my eyes

Grow heavy," Eva said; "they swim with
    sleep;
I cannot walk for utter weariness,
And I must rest a moment on this bank,
But let it not be long."   As thus she spoke,
In half-formed words, she sank on the smooth
    snow,
With closing lids. Her guide composed the
    robe
About her limbs, and said, " A pleasant spot
Is this to slumber in ; on such a couch
Oft have I slept away the winter night,
And had the sweetest dreams."   So Eva slept,
But slept in death ; for when the power of frost
Locks up the motions of the living frame,
The victim passes to the realm of Death
Through the dim porch of Sleep. The little
    guide,
Watching beside her, saw the hues of life
Fade from the fair smooth brow and rounded
    cheek,

As fades the crimson from a morning cloud,
Till they were white as marble, and the breath
Had ceased to come and go, yet knew she not
At first that this was death. But when she
     marked
How deep the paleness was, how motionless
That once lithe form, a fear came over her.
She strove to wake the sleeper, plucked her
     robe,
And shouted in her ear, but all in vain;
The life had passed away from those young
     limbs.
Then the snow-maiden raised a wailing cry,
Such as the dweller in some lonely wild,
Sleepless through all the long December night,
Hears when the mournful East begins to blow.

    But suddenly was heard the sound of steps,
Grating on the crisp snow; the cottagers
Were seeking Eva; from afar they saw
The twain, and hurried toward them. As they
    came,

    9*

With gentle chidings ready on their lips,
And marked that deathlike sleep, and heard the
      tale
Of the snow-maiden, mortal anguish fell
Upon their hearts, and bitter words of grief
And blame were uttered: " Cruel, cruel one,
To tempt our daughter thus, and cruel we,
Who suffered her to wander forth alone
In this fierce cold." They lifted the dear
      child,
And bore her home and chafed her tender
      limbs,
And strove, by all the simple arts they knew,
To make the chilled blood move, and win the
      breath
Back to her bosom; fruitlessly they strove.
The little maid was dead. In blank despair
They stood, and gazed at her who never more
Should look on them. " Why die we not with
      her ? "
They said; " without her life is bitterness."

Now came the funeral day; the simple folk
Of all that pastoral region gathered round,
To share the sorrow of the cottagers.
They carved a way into the mound of snow
To the glen's side, and dug a little grave
In the smooth slope, and, following the bier,
In long procession from the silent door,
Chanted a sad and solemn melody.

"Lay her away to rest within the ground.
Yea, lay her down whose pure and innocent
    life
Was spotless as these snows; for she was
    reared
In love, and passed in love life's pleasant
    spring,
And all that now our tenderest love can do
Is to give burial to her lifeless limbs."

They paused. A thousand slender voices
    round,
Like echoes softly flung from rock and hill,
Took up the strain, and all the hollow air

Seemed mourning for the dead; for, on that
    day,
The Little People of the Snow had come,
From mountain peak, and cloud, and icy hall,
To Eva's burial. As the murmur died
The funeral train renewed the solemn chant.
    "Thou, Lord, hast taken her to be with
    Eve,
Whose gentle name was given her. Even so,
For so Thy wisdom saw that it was best
For her and us. We bring our bleeding hearts,
And ask the touch of healing from Thy hand,
As, with submissive tears, we render back
The lovely and beloved to Him who gave."
    They ceased. Again the plaintive mur-
    mur rose.
From shadowy skirts of low-hung cloud it
    came,
And wide white fields, and fir-trees capped
    with snow,
Shivering to the sad sounds. They sank away
To silence in the dim-seen distant woods.

The little grave was closed; the funeral
    train
Departed; winter wore away; the spring
Steeped, with her quickening rains, the violet
    tufts,
By fond hands planted where the maiden
    slept.
But, after Eva's burial, never more
The Little People of the Snow were seen
By human eye, nor ever human ear
Heard from their lips, articulate speech
    again;
For a decree went forth to cut them off,
Forever, from communion with mankind.
The winter clouds, along the mountain-side,
Rolled downward toward the vale, but no fair
    form
Leaned from their folds, and, in the icy glens,
And aged woods, under snow-loaded pines,
Where once they made their haunt, was emp-
    tiness.

But ever, when the wintry days drew near,
Around that little grave, in the long night,
Frost-wreaths were laid and tufts of silvery
    rime
In shape like blades and blossoms of the field,
As one would scatter flowers upon a bier.

THE POET.

Thou, who wouldst wear the name
    Of poet mid thy brethren of mankind,
And clothe in words of flame
    Thoughts that shall live within the general
        mind!
Deem not the framing of a deathless lay
The pastime of a drowsy summer day.

But gather all thy powers,
    And wreak them on the verse that thou dost
        weave,
And in thy lonely hours,
    At silent morning or at wakeful eve,

While the warm current tingles through thy
    veins,
Set forth the burning words in fluent strains.

No smooth array of phrase,
    Artfully sought and ordered though it be,
Which the cold rhymer lays
    Upon his page with languid industry,
Can wake the listless pulse to livelier speed,
Or fill with sudden tears the eyes that read.

The secret wouldst thou know
    To touch the heart or fire the blood at will?
Let thine own eyes o'erflow;
    Let thy lips quiver with the passionate
        thrill;
Seize the great thought, ere yet its power be
        past,
And bind, in words, the fleet emotion fast.

Then, should thy verse appear
    Halting and harsh, and all unaptly wrought,
Touch the crude line with fear,
    Save in the moment of impassioned thought;
Then summon back the original glow and
        mend
The strain with rapture that with fire was
        penned.

Yet let no empty gust
    Of passion find an utterance in thy lay,
A blast that whirls the dust
    Along the howling street and dies away ;
But feelings of calm power and mighty sweep,
Like currents journeying through the windless
        deep.

Seek'st thou, in living lays,
    To limn the beauty of the earth and sky ?
Before thine inner gaze
    Let all that beauty in clear vision lie ;

Look on it with exceeding love, and write
The words inspired by wonder and delight.

Of tempests wouldst thou sing,
    Or tell of battles—make thyself a part
Of the great tumult; cling
    To the tossed wreck with terror in thy heart;
Scale, with the assaulting host, the rampart's
        height,
And strike and struggle in the thickest fight.

So shalt thou frame a lay
    That haply may endure from age to age,
And they who read shall say:
    What witchery hangs upon this poet's page!
What art is his the written spells to find
That sway from mood to mood the willing
        mind!

NOTES.

NOTES.

Page 40.

THE LOST BIRD.

READERS who are acquainted with the Spanish language may not be displeased at seeing the original of this little poem:

EL PAJARO PERDIDO.

Huyó con veielo incierto,
   Y de mis ojos ha desparecido,
Mirad, si, á vuestro huerto,
   Mi pajaro querido,
      Niñas hermosas, por acaso ha huido.

Sus ojos relucientes
    Son como los del aguila orgullosa;
Plumas resplandecientes,
    En la cabeza ariosa,
    Lleva; y su voz es tierna y armoniosa.

Mirad, si cuidadoso
    Junto á las flores se escondió en la grama.
Ese laurel frondoso
    Mirad, rama por rama,
    Que él los laureles y les flores ama.

Si le hallais, per ventura,
    No os enamore su amoroso acento;
No os prende su hermosura;
    Volvedmele al momento;
    O dejadle, si no, libre en el viento.

Por que su pico de oro
    Solo en mi mano toma la semilla;
Y no enjugaré el lloro
    Que veis en mi mejilla,
    Hasta encontrar mi profugo avecilla.

Mi vista se oscurece,
  Si sus ojos no vé, que son mi dia.
Mi ánima desfallece
  Con la melancolia
  De no escucharle ya su melodia.

The literature of Spain at the present day has this
peculiarity, that female writers have, in considerable
number, entered into competition with the other sex.
One of the most remarkable of these, as a writer of both
prose and poetry, is Carolina Coronado de Perry, the author of the little poem here given. The poetical literature of Spain has felt the influence of the female mind
in the infusion of a certain delicacy and tenderness, and
the more frequent choice of subjects which interest the
domestic affections. Concerning the verses of the lady
already mentioned, Don Juan Eugenio Hartzenbusch,
one of the most accomplished Spanish critics of the present day, and himself a successful dramatic writer, says:

  "If Carolina Coronado had, through modesty, sent
her productions from Estremadura to Madrid under the
name of a person of the other sex, it would still have
been difficult for intelligent readers to persuade themselves that they were written by a man, or at least, con-

sidering their graceful sweetness, purity of tone, simplicity
of conception, brevity of development, and delicate and
particular choice of subject, we should be constrained to
attribute them to one yet in his early youth, whom the
imagination would represent as ingenuous, innocent and
gay, who had scarce ever wandered beyond the flowery
grove or pleasant valley where his cradle was rocked,
and where he had been lulled to sleep by the sweetest
songs of Francisco de la Torre, Garcilaso and Melendez."

The author of the *Pajaro Perdido*, according to a me-
moir of her by Angel Fernandez do los Rios, was born
at Almendralejo, in Estremadura, in 1823. At the age
of nine years she began to steal from sleep, after a day
passed in various lessons, and in domestic occupations,
several hours every night to read the poets of her country, and other books belonging to the library of the
household, among which is mentioned as a proof of
her vehement love of reading, the Critical History of
Spain, by the Abbé Masuden, "and other works equally
dry and prolix." She was afterwards sent to Badajoz,
where she received the best education which the state of
the country, then on fire with a civil war, would admit.
Here the intensity of her application to her studies
caused a severe malady, which has frequently recurred

in after life. At the age of thirteen years she wrote a poem entitled *La Palma*, which the author of her biography declares to be worthy of Herrera, and which led Espronceda, a poet of Estremadura, a man of genius, and the author of several translations from Byron, whom he resembled both in mental and personal characteristics, to address her an eulogistic sonnet. In 1843, when she was but twenty years old, a volume of her poems was published at Madrid, in which were included both that entitled *La Palma*, and the one I have given in this note. To this volume Hartzenbusch, in his admiration for her genius, prefaced an introduction.

The task of writing verses in Spanish is not difficult. Rhymes are readily found, and the language is easily moulded into metrical forms. Those who have distinguished themselves in this literature have generally made their first essays in verse. What is remarkable enough, the men who afterwards figure in political life mostly begin their career as the authors of madrigals. A poem introduces the future statesman to the public, as a speech at a popular meeting introduces the candidate for political distinction in this country. I have heard of but one of the eminent Spanish politicians of the present time, who made a boast that he was innocent of poetry, and if all

10

that his enemies say of him be true, it would have been well both for his country and his own fame, if he had been equally innocent of corrupt practices. The compositions of Carolina Coronado, even her earliest, do not deserve to be classed with the productions of which we have spoken, and which are simply the effect of inclination and facility. They possess the *mens divinior*.

In 1852 a collection of the poems of Carolina Coronado was brought out at Madrid, including those which were first published. The subjects are of larger variety than those which prompted her earlier productions; some of them are of a religious cast, others refer to political matters. One of them, which appears among the "Improvisations," is an energetic protest against erecting a new amphitheatre for bull-fights. The spirit of all her poetry is humane and friendly to the best interests of mankind.

Her writings in prose must not be overlooked. Among them is a novel entitled *Sigea*, founded on the adventures of Camoens; another entitled *Jorilla*, a beautiful story, full of pictures of rural life in Estremadura, which deserves, if it could find a competent translator, to be transferred to our language. Besides these there are two other novels from her pen, *Paquita* and *La Luz del*

Tejo. A few years since appeared, in a Madrid periodi-
cal, the *Semanario,* a series of letters written by her, giv-
ing an account of the impressions received in a journey
from the Tagus to the Rhine, including a visit to Eng-
land. Among the subjects on which she has written, is
the idea, still warmly cherished in Spain, of uniting the
entire peninsula under one government. In an ably con-
ducted journal of Madrid, she has given accounts of the
poetesses of Spain, her contemporaries, with extracts
from their writings, and a kindly estimate of their re-
spective merits.

Her biographer speaks of her activity and efficiency
in charitable enterprises, her interest in the cause of
education, her visits to the primary schools of Madrid,
encouraging and rewarding the pupils, and her patron-
age of the *escuela de parvulos,* or infant school, at Badajoz, established by a society in that city, with the design
of improving the education of the laboring class.

It must have been not long after the publication of
her poems, in 1852, that Carolina Coronado became the
wife of an American gentleman, Mr. Horatio J. Perry, at
one time our Secretary of Legation at the Court of Madrid, afterwards our *Chargé d'Affaires,* and now, in 1863,
again Secretary of Legation. Amidst the duties of a wife

and mother, which she fulfils with exemplary fidelity and grace, she has not either forgotten or forsaken the literary pursuits which have given her so high a reputation.

Page 90.

THE RUINS OF ITALICA.

The poems of the Spanish author, Francisco de Rioja, who lived in the first half of the seventeenth century, are few in number, but much esteemed. His ode on the Ruins of Italica is one of the most admired of these, but in the only collection of his poems which I have seen, it is said that the concluding stanza, in the original copy, was deemed so little worthy of the rest that it was purposely omitted in the publication. Italica was a city founded by the Romans in the South of Spain, the remains of which are still an object of interest.

Page 118.

SELLA.

Sella is the name given by the Vulgate to one of the wives of Lamech, mentioned in the fourth chapter of the Book of Genesis, and called Zillah in the common English version of the Bible.

Page 150.

It may be esteemed presumptuous in the author of this volume to attempt a translation of any part of Homer in blank verse after that of Cowper. It has always seemed to him, however, that Cowper's version had very great defects. The style of Homer is simple, and he has been praised for fire and rapidity of narrative. Does any body find these qualities in Cowper's Homer? If Cowper had rendered him into such English as he employed in his "Task," there would be no reason to complain; but in translating Homer he seems to have thought it necessary to use a different style from that of his original works. Almost every sentence is stiffened by some clumsy inversion; stately phrases are used when simpler ones were at hand, and would have rendered the meaning of the original better. The entire version has the appearance of being hammered out with great labor, and as a whole it is cold and constrained; scarce anything seems spontaneous; it is only now and then that the translator has caught the fervor of his author. Homer, of course, wrote in idiomatic Greek, and, in order to produce either a true copy of the original or an agreeable poem, should have been translated into idiomatic English.

I am almost ashamed, after this censure of an author, whom, in the main, I admire so much as I do Cowper, to refer to my own translation of the Fifth Book of the Odyssey.   I desire barely to say that I have endeavored to give the verses of the old Greek poet at least a simpler presentation in English, and one more conformable to the genius of our language.

THE END.